MYSTERIUM ③

THE WHEEL OF
LIFE AND DEATH

JULIAN SEDGWICK

CAROLRHODA BOOKS
Minneapolis

First American edition published in 2018 by Carolrhoda Books

Text copyright © Julian Sedgwick, 2014
First published in Great Britain in 2014 by Hodder Children's Books, a division of
Hachette Children's Books, an Hatchette UK company

Cover illustration by Patricia Moffett
Cover illustration copyright © 2018 by Lerner Publishing Group, Inc.

Carolrhoda Books
A division of Lerner Publishing Group, Inc.
241 First Avenue North
Minneapolis, MN 55401 USA

For reading levels and more information, look up this title at www.lernerbooks.com.

Map, skull, and code chart © Laura Westlund/Independent Picture Service.

Main body text set in Bembo Std 12.5/17.
Typeface provided by Monotype Typography.

Library of Congress Cataloging-in-Publication Data

The Cataloging-in-Publication Data for *The Wheel of Life and Death* is on file at the
Library of Congress.
ISBN 978-1-4677-7569-4 (trade hardcover)
ISBN 978-1-5124-9849-3 (eb pdf)

LC record available at https://lccn.loc.gov/2017004653

Manufactured in the United States of America
1-37419-18417-5/15/2017

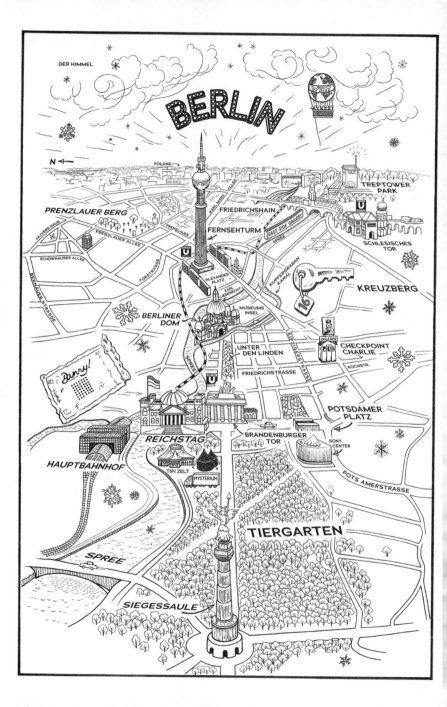

PRAISE FOR
THE BLACK DRAGON
BOOK 1 OF THE MYSTERIUM TRILOGY

"This first installment in the Mysterium series is filled with action
and stage magic, though Danny's struggles with identity and
his parents' deaths are never far from the surface, making this
adventure more than gangster brawls and misdirection."
—*Booklist*

"A clever mashup of crime drama and magical realism
makes for an auspicious series start."
—*Kirkus Reviews*

"Gripping series introduction."
—*School Library Journal*

PRAISE FOR
THE PALACE OF MEMORY
BOOK 2 OF THE MYSTERIUM TRILOGY

"Sedgwick keeps the pages turning with nonstop action;
daring circus stunts; light mystery; and an interesting,
multiethnic cast of characters."
—*Booklist*

"A thrilling read."
—*Kirkus Reviews*

"Danny's charm, abilities, and mental fortitude will
endear him to both old and new readers."
—*School Library Journal*

FOR MY BROTHER

ACT ONE

SEEING A FEARLESS ACROBAT IN BRIGHT
COSTUME, WE FORGET OURSELVES,
FEELING WE HAVE SOMEHOW RISEN
ABOVE AND REACHED THE LEVEL OF
UNIVERSAL STRENGTH.

—*Karl Marx*

1

WHEN THE BLOOD IS PUMPING

Danny knows he has to move.

But he can't. His body—tired, drugged, shocked—refuses to obey. Beneath his feet, far below the roof of the cathedral, the city has stuck fast. As if it were a mechanism, tightly wound with pent-up energy, waiting for someone to flick a switch and set it all whirring back into life.

There's no sound, no movement. Just his hands clamped to the metal of the crane jib, his knuckles showing white, his heart thrumming in his ears and that profound expanse of nothingness waiting to devour him.

Even the parakeets have gone silent in the trees below.

The relentless pace of the last few days has taken its toll on his physical self—and now, for a moment, his mind is stalling too. The full moon hangs motionless, pinned to the dark sky over Barcelona, and the aircraft-warning beacon on top of the crane blinks away hypnotically. He feels like he's floating, as if he could just let go and drift: an astronaut on a space walk.

"Danny?" A panicked voice, filtering into his consciousness. "Danny! Keep moving! Just a few rungs more."

He looks up to see Sing Sing reaching out toward him, her oval face creased with concern, imploring him to make that last effort to reach safety. Darko Blanco looms behind her—but his gaze is *down*, into the trees below, into the abyss that has just swallowed the assassin, La Loca.

"Darko! Help me! Danny's frozen."

The knife thrower snaps to attention. "I'll get him. Don't worry." Making sure of his handholds on the skeletal arm of the crane, he edges forward.

Behind Darko there's another figure now—the twitch of a silhouetted Mohawk: Aki has reached the crane cab and is shouting his encouragement. And Bjorn is close behind, moonlight flashing on the skull mask tipped back on his head.

"It's OK," Danny manages to say. "Just felt a bit woozy."

He glances down again, swallows the panic, and then looks toward Darko and Sing Sing, toward safety.

Got to shake it, he thinks. *Got to move.* It would be stupid to fail now.

With a massive effort of will, he unclamps his right hand.

"That's it, kiddo," Darko says, glancing back over his shoulder. "Take your time."

Danny nods. The paralysis is easing and he takes a step, shoe gripping metal, horribly aware of just how high up they are. *I hardly noticed it while I was trying to escape La Loca,* he thinks. *Must have been the buzz of adrenaline.*

Aki's joined Darko and they're both encouraging him to keep moving. But as he takes another step, the coordination drops from his limbs—and he slips, missing the framework. He lurches down, hands scrabbling for hold, his right foot shooting out into space, treading thin air.

"Dannnnyyyyyyy . . . !"

Sing Sing's shriek jolts his system, waking his reflexes—just in time to see Darko reach out toward him. Danny throws out his left hand, grabs for the knife thrower—and their palms slap each other's forearms, locked in a tight circus grip. The force of the catch jars through him, yanking at his shoulder, shaking loose one of his trainers, and it falls, somersaulting down and down. For a full second—it seems like a minute—he watches it go, his stomach in his mouth, his heart going full speed. Then Darko is heaving him up, using all the strength in his wiry, athletic frame to pull him onto the safety of the walkway nearer the cab.

"I've got you."

Danny's eyes, firing green and brown, return Darko's gaze.

The knife thrower looks ashen-faced. Aki has a firm grip round his waist, leaning back as if steadying a flier on the trapeze.

"I thought I was going to fall," Danny murmurs.

The knife thrower smiles. "Not this time! Thanks to Aki."

"And you, Darko," Sing Sing chirrups. She throws her arms around Danny, fighting back the tears.

"I'm OK," he says, breathing heavily. His eyes rove across the city spread out around them—and he sees that it's moving again.

The switch has been thrown—and life has returned, the nighttime traffic circulating, pumping blood in the veins of the city, mopeds and taxis surging around the Sagrada Familia. A jet grinds overhead, scoring its silver trail across the sky—and then, from inside the cathedral itself, there's the sound of music throbbing. And applause—wild applause—and whistling and cheers. The show coming to an end.

Danny reaches for his back pocket. Yes, safely there! The sheets with Dad's coded communication, crackling away—two of his messages from beyond the grave still waiting to be deciphered. *There's no time to waste*, he thinks. *With each moment that passes we could be falling behind the Forty-Nine, losing ground. We need to take the initiative.*

"OK," he says. "Let's get down."

2

WHEN FEISTY RING-MISTRESSES 'FESS UP

Half an hour later, the whole company is gathered in the performance space. The audience has gone—still not quite sure what they've witnessed: buzzing and elated by Danny's escape high above their heads, but confused by the reaction of the other members of the troupe, by the chaotic finish as Rosa jumped from her flaming Cyr wheel and ran off without taking the applause.

Now the cathedral broods in darkness around them. Danny has pulled away from the others and is perched on a flight case, his back half-turned for privacy. He's scribbling hurriedly on the sheets of paper, trying to place the keyword for code 2. Who knows what the message will reveal? Whatever it says, he wants a moment to himself to react before he shows it to anyone else.

But he's struggling to make it work. He's only recently emerged from a drug-induced sleep—La Loca's work—and his head's still fogged. He glances up now to try and clear it. The Sagrada Familia's pillars disappear into the emptiness above, and with a shiver, he remembers that fight to get clear of the suffocating grip of the straitjacket. Need to *breeeeathe.*

The company is gathered around Rosa, heatedly debating what to do next, everyone talking at once. Danny turns to listen and sees Sing Sing hovering halfway between him and the group, casting suspicious, dark eyes at the ringmistress.

"I should turn myself over to the police," Darko declares, his east European accent thickening like it does on the rare occasions when he's stressed. "Explain what happened—hope for the best."

"No way!" Bjorn growls. "That maniac was going to kill Danny. Darko saved him. We need to find the body, retrieve the knife—and then get out of here."

"Besides," Aki nods, "not sure we can trust the police. Not after what happened to Danny and Sing Sing."

Major Zamora, his arm bound stiffly to his side, shakes his head. "There are plenty of good police in Barcelona. Just because there are a few bad apples, it doesn't mean they're all rotten—"

"I'll go with the decision of the group," Darko cuts in. "But I'm not keen on any time in prison."

"But the body will be found," Zamora rumbles, "and it will have a Dubé throwing knife in it with your prints all over—"

"Quiet!" Rosa barks. "I can't hear myself think. We've got to protect the company, protect the *bambini*."

"Who are you calling *bambini*?" Sing Sing snaps, turning away to look for support from Danny. Her quick smile is meant to reassure, but there's something awkward in it too. Reserved.

Something's not quite right with Sing Sing since we got down off the crane, he thinks. But it'll have to wait—the most urgent thing is to crack this code.

He looks back at the wrinkled piece of paper, refocusing. His first attempts at placing the keyword in the rail fence grid have resulted in gibberish. Now he studies the code itself, picking out the high-frequency numbers, and makes another stab at putting the letters of MYSTERIUM on the first line. You ignore any duplicate—in this case the second M—and then run the remaining alphabet after that . . .

0	1	2	3	4	5	6	7	8	9
M	Y	S	T	E	R	I	U		
8	A	B	C	D	F	G	H	J	K	L
9	N	O	P	Q	V	W	X	Z		

He checks the first chunk of code once again. And yes! It's working this time . . .

THINKJIMMY . . . THINK JIMMY . . . Engrossed now, the argument slipping from his attention, he works quickly to unlock Dad's message.

38669 08887 600|8 26838 99|82 8829|
90958 03458 248989–8|738 64629 09|33
86482 490345!

The excitement builds as he sees the words forming. It feels like a kind of miracle: Dad speaking to him again, helping him, pointing him the right way.

THINKJIMMYDIDTHELOCKS . . .

So our suspicions were right! Jimmy Torrini, former company member—he sabotaged Dad's trick and almost killed him.

There's someone at Danny's shoulder now, a shadow falling on the paper. Instinctively, he hides what he's doing, but then—seeing it's Sing Sing—he lifts his hand to uncover what he's revealed so far. *If I keep showing her how much I trust her*, he thinks, *maybe that will help smooth over any problem between us. She must be feeling really awful after finding out that Mum abandoned her . . .*

"Just like you thought," Sing Sing whispers. "You've got to challenge Rosa."

"Wait a minute."

As fast as he can, he unpicks the last groups of numbers.

BUTHEISNOTTHECENTER

Sing Sing squints at the full message and raises her eyebrows. "If Jimmy tried to kill your dad once, why not twice?"

"And I remember seeing Jimmy," Danny says. "The night of the fire. We know he had a motive too. Revenge."

He turns to look at the ringmistress. She's standing in the middle of the company, holding her hands up like a policewoman trying to direct unruly traffic.

At the very least, she's been economical with the truth! It's time to confront her. The tiredness in his legs has gone now, replaced by renewed determination and urgency, and he strides toward Rosa. *Need to pitch this just right*, he thinks. *Need to sound and look strong. Can't risk messing up this chance.*

But as soon as he moves, he has everyone's attention. All eyes are fixed on his. They can see the intensity there—and the memory of the escape from the burning rope is still strong in their minds, putting genuine respect into each face.

Danny senses he's taking center stage again, and his confidence falters for a moment. But then he dismisses the thought. The golden rule of performance: if you don't feel it, then fake it. Fake it as hard as you can until you do feel it.

He marches up to the ringmistress and rustles the paper in front of her nose, invading her space, taking control. His voice, when it comes, is as deep as he can manage. "It was Jimmy T who sabotaged the water torture cell, wasn't it?"

"I—" Rosa clamps her mouth shut and shakes her head.

He nods very slightly, just enough to encourage her.

"It was Jimmy, and you . . . knew . . . all . . . along." Rosa's eyes are trying to dart away, but he's got a grip on them now.

"Danny, I—"

"Tell me about Jimmy. I know he was there. You were hiding something the night of the fire, when you found me in the prop trailer. What was it?"

The silence deepens. Just the sound of Herzog's claws on the flagstones as he comes to stand beside Danny. The ringmistress screws up her mouth, trying to hold onto the words, one red rose still tangled in her hair.

She pulls it out now—and then her shoulders sag.

"Well, come on, Rosa Vega. Spit it out," Zamora says.

Danny's gaze is unwavering. He can see the truth is forcing its way out. She can't hold onto it, can't cope with containing the guilt anymore—and his heart quickens in anticipation.

"OK," Rosa says, prying her eyes away to look at the flower crumpled in her hands. "Yes. It was Jimmy who fiddled with the water cell—"

There are groans of dismay from the others, but Rosa holds up her hand. "Listen! He didn't want to *hurt* your dad, Danny, I'm sure of that—just give him a bit of a fright and embarrass him. He was all messed up by his feelings for your mamma!"

At last, an admission! An important piece of the mystery slotting into place. Danny struggles to keep his excitement—and anger—in check. He doesn't want to lose this precious momentum.

"So why didn't *you* say anything?"

"Because I thought people would jump to con-clusions. The wrong conclusions! I didn't even know what he was going to do until he came rushing up after the show and gave me the mask and the trousers with the paint on them. That's why I was in the prop store—I was going to get some paraffin and burn them. Poor Jimmy—"

"Poor Jimmy? Yeah, right," Zamora rumbles. "He broke the golden rule! And he's *got* to be the one who started the fire then!"

"No!" Rosa says, shaking her head. "He was back in New York that night. I phoned him there. Told him never to come near the Mysterium again. The fire *must* have been an accident—"

13

Danny throws his hands up. "No way was it an accident. Not after everything else that's happened. I *saw* Jimmy that night."

"But you can't have, *Bello*. Maybe the emotion of it all has played a trick on your mind."

Darko raises his eyebrows. "Maybe we *should* keep an open mind—"

"He was in New York," Rosa repeats. "And he can't be involved in what happened tonight either. Why would Jimmy want to hurt Danny—or Zamora—or Sing Sing? It makes no sense!"

The silence returns now—profound, troubled—as everyone tries to digest the new information: Jimmy, a saboteur. And Rosa, the director of the company, keeping it secret! *Maybe it's the end for the company*, Danny thinks, heart sinking.

"I hate to press," Darko says, "but I'd like to resolve my problem. What do you think we should do, Danny? You seem to be the only person keeping his—or her—head around here."

Danny's gaze flicks from one member of the company to the other, and he sees they're all waiting for an answer—the whole company looking his way, expecting him to offer leadership again. *Must have faked it pretty well,* he thinks, shutting his eyes. *I ought to pick the problem apart, use Dad's "atomic method" and consider each bit, one by one.*

But instinct is taking over, already pushing him to a decision. He knows he's about to cross a line—bending the truth, messing with a crime scene—but Darko saved his life, after all. He doesn't deserve to languish in a jail cell while the Mysterium moves on.

"We need to find La Loca," Danny says. "Make sure she's . . ." his voice falters. "We'll get Darko's knife back. Then call the police and say she fell. Assuming she hasn't already been found. And maybe the knife got knocked out when she fell through the trees." He turns back to Rosa. "But then you're all going to help me track Jimmy down."

The ringmistress looks crestfallen, uncertain. "What do you think, Zamora?"

"We've lived on the edge before . . ." he puffs out his cheeks. "But I'm drafting in some extra help. Security."

"Let's vote then," Rosa says briskly, trying to regain some authority. "Who's in favor?"

All hands rise into the air—apart from Darko's. "I'm abstaining," he mumbles.

"Good!" The ringmistress claps her hands together. "That's decided." She hesitates and then turns to Danny. "Forgive me, *Bello*. I should have told you. But I was very fond of Jimmy—"

"Just help me track him down. Promise we'll do that—"

"On my family honor, I promise," Rosa says. She puts her right hand on her heart, holds his gaze for a moment, then stalks off to supervise the others.

Sing Sing tugs at Danny's elbow. "You're letting her off that easy?"

"I need Rosa's help. The others are going to give her a hard enough time. And I need to get hold of Inspector Ricard and ask him what he thinks. Ask him about Jimmy."

Maybe the Interpol man has more information by now. Maybe he'll be able to warn them what's coming next. La Loca was just a hired gun, after all—and even if the Forty-Nine are routed here in Barcelona, the rest of them are still out there, waiting. At their heart, Center is still to be uncovered, confronted, defeated.

"What about this lot?" Sing Sing says, jerking her head at the company behind them. "All clear?"

"I think so. What Javier said about someone being linked to the company—that must have meant Jimmy . . ."

He frowns. Something else is worrying him. "Sing Sing—do you think we're doing the right thing about Darko's knife?"

"Only an idiot thinks everything's black and white, Danny."

"But—"

"But nothing."

Herzog's sniffing away at Danny's shoeless foot, and Sing Sing puts her hand on the dog's shaggy head. "There's a Chinese proverb. It says a good dog and a bad dog are fighting inside us. You just have to make sure to feed the good dog enough so that he wins in the end . . ." She turns away. "You've fed your good dog a lot. Even if this time you're throwing a scrap to the bad boy . . ."

Danny waits impatiently for the search party to return.

But when—thirty long minutes later—he sees the Klowns, Maria, Frankie, and Darko come back into the cathedral, there's no urgency at all in their stride. All six of them look baffled.

"We split up and looked everywhere under that crane arm," Frankie calls. "And a good bit farther too. Maria and Aki shimmied up the trees in case she was wedged there . . ."

"And?" Danny asks eagerly.

"Not a trace of her," Darko says. "No body, no coat, no blood, no knife. Nothing. Just this in the middle of a path!" He dangles Danny's missing shoe on one long finger.

"In which case," Rosa says, relief brightening her voice, "there's nothing really to report, is there?"

"But she can't have survived, can she?" Danny says. "We have to be sure. Maybe she's been taken away by the police already—"

"I don't think so," Frankie says, scratching his bald head. "There's no crime-scene tape or nothing. Maybe she landed on the roof somewhere."

Rosa sighs. "So forget her!"

"But we can't just ignore it," Danny presses. Rosa's judgment is in question, after all—and it doesn't feel right to walk away from this problem without resolving it.

The ringmistress reaches up to rub the back of her neck. "Look, *Bello*. We'll just work through tomorrow's show, do a lightning teardown, and then get on the road. If anything crops up in the next twenty-four hours, we'll deal with it."

Darko hands Danny his shoe. "Rosa's right. Nothing else we can do now."

Danny sighs impatiently, then bends to tie his laces. "And where are we going next?"

"We're going to Berlin," Rosa says quietly.

The breath catches in his chest. "Berlin?"

"We're at Zirkus Berlin Festival for a week. You'll have to come with us—so we can keep you safe until your aunt's out of prison."

Berlin.

The news snuffs out all other thoughts for a moment: Aunt Laura's predicament, the mystery of La Loca's missing body, whatever it is that's bugging Sing Sing. It's as if a cold wind has struck his face.

Berlin!

For him the place now stands for just one moment: the night of Mum and Dad's deaths. That all-consuming fire. It stands for danger, the end of things.

And it means that he will have to make a journey he's been both dreading and knowing that he needs to take. The long journey to stand—at last—by his parents' graveside.

3

WHEN THERE ARE STRANGE VOICES IN THE NIGHT

That single name is still ringing in Danny's ears as later that night he, Zamora, and Sing Sing huddle around the table in Rosa's caravan. It's as if a voice is repeating it quietly over and over again, his heart beat emphasizing the syllables.

Ber-lin, Ber-lin, Ber-lin.

The curtains are drawn tightly against the world outside, and Danny's glad of it as he tries to concentrate on what Zamora is saying.

The dwarf rips open a packet of pills. "We're not taking any more chances. I've got two of Javier's best men standing guard for us until we get out of here. They look like a couple of jokers—Tweedledum and

Tweedledee, Javier called them—but they're decent. Tough too." He chucks two painkillers into his mouth and gulps them down without water, grimacing.

"But are they trustworthy?" Sing Sing says, parting the curtains. Danny peers over her shoulder into the sliver of darkness. They can just make out the burly form of one of the two brothers, a shadow under the mountainous cathedral, his curly-haired head scanning the night for trouble.

"*Sí, sí*. I'm sure of that," Zamora says, waving the thought away. "I know those boys so well. Used to change their diapers—"

"But you were wrong about Javier," Danny snaps. He needs all the help he can get, and it's fast becoming clear that he can't rely on the adults around him.

Zamora's eyes flash, and he opens his mouth to reply—but then shuts it again. He reaches out his good arm and plants his hand on Danny's shoulder, squeezing it, seeking out the boy's eyes.

"We're all just doing our best, Danny. You know that. And nobody's going to get past me again and try to hurt you—not while there's breath in me."

Danny manages half a smile in reply. But where before he felt he could rely on Zamora—the great Major Pablo Zamora Lopez, dwarf strongman and daredevil, the rock of the company—now that confidence has been well and truly shaken. *I don't doubt his loyalty,* Danny thinks. *Just his judgment. His radar.*

"Maybe we're in the clear for now," Sing Sing says. "I don't think those Forty-Nine goons will be up for anything. They were in bad shape when we saw them last—"

"Worse," Zamora says through gritted teeth. "The boys tell me the van blew up. Two of them didn't make it out."

Sing Sing whistles. "Good riddance."

But Danny is feeling sick to his stomach. *We're responsible for that,* he thinks. *I was just trying to stop the van, to escape. But if I hadn't blinded the driver with the flashlight . . . ?*

"I didn't mean them to get hurt," he says under his breath.

Sing Sing shakes her head impatiently. "People who play with fire get burned—and that's that. OK?"

Danny slumps in his seat. *Maybe,* he thinks. *But it feels like we just gave that bad dog a decent meal.*

"I've got an appointment at the hospital tomorrow afternoon," Zamora says. "They need to put the proper cast on. Until then I'm not letting you out of my sight, Danny. We'll take sleeping bags and bed down in the prop store. I can't stay with Lope—not with what she's going through after losing Javier—and all her family are there already. You keep me company. And vice versa, no?"

Always my hideout in the old days, Danny thinks. But now it's so very different—and he wants to keep close to Sing Sing. Talk to her about the discovery of the birth certificate and what it means for them both. Provided she's willing to talk . . .

After the immediate rush of the rescue and recovery, she's definitely holding back, withdrawing inside that prickly shell again. And it's going to take time for Danny to get used to the fact that she's his half sister. *What should I call her now? Sing Sing? Half sister? Sis?*

They look different—there's no denying it. His tangle of Welsh, English, and Chinese genes makes him look Asian when surrounded by Westerners, and European in the streets of Kowloon. Sing Sing is Chinese through and through, from her straight, black hair to the tips of her toes. But there's certainly that resemblance to Mum. Weird how he can easily see the similarity in her eyes now, in the curve of her mouth.

"Danny?" Zamora presses.

"I'll stay with you, Sing Sing. If you want—"

"Don't worry about me. I can make sure there's nothing else Rosa isn't telling us about the fire. Or about my mother!" Her voice snags on that last word, and she looks away hurriedly.

Zamora frowns. Despite the late hour, he's insisted on them recounting everything that happened in the park earlier—the discovery of Sing Sing's birth certificate, Dad's copy of the Proust book. Now he chews the knuckles of his good hand, glancing at the contents of the package, thinking hard. "Proust!" he splutters. "Why Proust, of all things?"

Danny shakes his head. "I don't know! Maybe he just wanted me to read it."

"Got to be more than that. Here, show me that birth certificate again," he says. "My eyes popped out of my head when I saw it the first time."

But Sing Sing doesn't answer. She just keeps staring out into the darkness, her shoulders hunched.

"Look, you two," she mumbles after a long silence. "I want to keep this between ourselves for now. I feel kind of embarrassed. Stupid—"

"But you shouldn't," Danny says, reaching to put a hand on her shoulder. "I mean—"

"That's what I want," she snaps. "Can't you

understand I'm trying to process something pretty flipping tricky here?"

Slowly, Danny withdraws his hand. *Me too*, he thinks. *Me too.*

———————————

That gap opening between them gnaws away at Danny as he tries to get comfortable in the prop trailer. He's been drifting in and out of sleep for an hour or so—but despite his extreme exhaustion, he can't switch off. *Why did Mum abandon Sing Sing? Why didn't they tell me about her?* It should be snug in here with Zamora for company—at boarding school he would have grabbed this moment with both hands—but now it's impossible to feel at ease. The thought of Berlin is ticking away, and however much he tries to shut it out, he keeps seeing La Loca: that blank look as the knife struck her, then that long plummet into the void.

Now somewhere far away a clock is striking two. *It's no good*, Danny thinks, *I can't sleep—and I'm really thirsty.* His mouth feels like an old carpet—has ever since he came back to consciousness at the end of the burning rope. There's nothing to drink in here, but one of the trailers is normally loaded with provisions and bottled water. Zamora is propped in a half-sitting position by the door, snoring, sleeping pills and exhaustion working together to drag him under. Without his trademark bowler hat, he looks vulnerable, the stubble on his balding head catching the dim light spilling through the hatch above. He turns restlessly in his sleep, eyelids twitching with some troubled dream.

As quietly as he can, Danny picks his way past Zamora, eases the door open, and lets himself out into the night.

A chill wind's blowing around the corner of the Sagrada, and the moon is dipping low in the sky. *I'll be as quick as I can*, he thinks. *Should be safe enough.*

From a nearby street, there's the clink of breaking glass and some laughter—but otherwise, nothing to be heard. Danny pulls the hood up on his Mysterium Crew sweatshirt and slips across the compound, past Darko's old red camper, the lighting truck where Frankie bunks, Rosa's caravan.

He thinks of Sing Sing tucked up in the caravan. *Is she asleep—or awake like me? Hope the discovery in the park won't mess up our friendship. It should make it deeper, shouldn't it?*

He's almost reached the provisions trailer—and then something catches his attention, worming its way into his thoughts. A high voice—steady, calm—barely audible. So indistinct at first that he thinks he's imagining it. But there it is again, repeating each short phrase twice, as if reciting dictation. He hears it quite distinctly for a few seconds: a young child listing what sound like numbers.

"*Vier . . . sieben . . . zwo . . . acht . . . acht. Vier sieben zwo acht acht. Neun . . . zwo . . . eins . . . sieben . . . drei. Neun zwo . . .*"

German? Strange coincidence when he's been thinking about Berlin for the last few hours! The words sound flat, two-dimensional, as if coming through a speaker—but it's impossible to work out where the sound is coming from—

And then an ambulance goes howling past, and by the time that's gone, there's nothing but the whisper of the breeze. *A weird kind of thing to be listening to,* he thinks, *maybe some kind of language lesson—*

Sudden footsteps ring out behind him, loud and very close, making him jump. As he spins round a nightmarish image flicks across his imagination: La Loca staggering toward him with that knife in the back of her neck, somehow still alive, still chasing him.

But instead, he finds himself face-to-face with the older of the Tweedle brothers standing guard. The man looms over him, his eyes shifting quickly left and right, sweeping the surroundings like someone who's used to looking out for trouble.

"Better keep in truck," he whispers, searching uncertainly for English. "I saw some *chico*—a man standing on the other side of the gate. Long time he stands there. I go to talk to him and he goes. Very quick. Tall guy, dark clothes. Probably just homeless guy, but Zamora says be careful, so . . ."

Danny glances in the direction the man is pointing. Nothing. Just a plastic bag caught in a mini-vortex, twitching and snapping. He feels a shiver bump the length of his spine. "Did you hear a voice just then? A child?"

The man shakes his head and points to the headphone cords snaking into his mass of curly hair. "Listening to my music," he says. "Good stuff." He holds out an earbud for Danny to hear, and the tinny beat fidgets in the air between them.

"I'd better get back to Zamora," Danny says.

The man nods. "Don't worry." He pats something bulky in his jacket pocket, then turns away to scan the dark spaces beyond the railings, his hand resting on whatever is hidden there. A gun? In one way that's reassuring—in another it just underlines how real the danger is.

Danny grabs a water from the provisions trailer, then hurries back into the cluster of vehicles, eager for the security they afford.

As he climbs back into the prop trailer, Zamora shifts in his sleeping bag, groaning in pain. Danny reaches down to put a hand on the dwarf's shoulder.

"Everything's OK, Major. You're sleeping now. Very deeply sleeping. Your arm is feeling better, much better—nice and easy—and you're sleeping peacefully . . ." Zamora's breathing hesitates, then shifts gear, becomes smoother—and his shoulders release a fraction. *If only someone could hypnotize me,* Danny thinks. *Then I could get some proper rest too. Or even find whatever else is lurking deeper in my memory. Maybe I could ask Darko? No—it wouldn't work. I'd second guess what he was doing, and I wouldn't really let go.*

Might as well work if I can't sleep . . .

He finds a headlamp hanging on the wall nearby and trains its light on the third clue. That brief message is the last thing Dad wrote. Its position in the notebook—the underlining, the urgency of the handwriting—all point to how much it must mean.

If the threat from the Forty-Nine can reach as far as Danny's school in England and Hong Kong and here to Barcelona, then he's in no doubt there'll be trouble ahead in Berlin. *The organization will have a cell there,* he thinks. *They may well be waiting for me.*

Vigorously, he shakes free of the thought. He's here now—and all that matters is to crack Dad's stupid clue. The other stuff can wait.

This one takes the biscuit. Remember?

No, he doesn't remember! It certainly doesn't look like another rail fence or substitution cypher. And then there are those faint smudges on the side of the page, as if Dad rubbed something out, there— and there. What could they have been? Something vital, or a trivial thought erased?

He holds the headlamp against the back of the sheet, the light glowing through the thin paper, the hazy marks—but they're still impossible to read. Maybe Ricard—or someone who works for him in Interpol—could help? Danny focuses the beam on the clue again, ransacking his memory for anything that will help unlock it. It feels like there's something familiar lying just out of reach in the back of his head. *Think!*

But nothing comes—and he stares at Dad's writing so long that eventually the words and numbers start to blur and swim before his eyes . . .

Zamora wakes with a start to see a square of daylight overhead. On the far side of the trailer, Danny's fast asleep, the headlamp shining from his forehead, the sheets of paper clutched in his hand.

The dwarf goes over and squints at them.

Around the third cypher and clue there is nothing new except a ring of increasingly urgent and frustrated question marks.

4

WHEN BUBBLES BURST

Morning sun rakes the Sagrada Familia's parking lot. Beyond the railings the stalls are ready for business, canopies fluttering in the breeze, the line of tourists already reaching round from the main entrance.

A young man in dreadlocks has a bowl of soapy water in front of him and is entertaining the waiting customers by dragging a hoop through the mixture, conjuring enormous bubbles. They float trembling into the morning air. One of them, its blue sheen shape-shifting, drifts on the breeze toward Danny, clips the spiked top of the railings—and blinks out of existence.

No sign yet of Sing Sing. But Darko is sitting in the open side door of his camper van, shoulders hunched, nursing a big cup of *café con leche*.

He looks up as Danny and Zamora come over, the light picking out the furrows on his face. His salt-and-pepper hair is disheveled, shirt more crumpled than usual.

"Morning," he sighs. "Anyone sleep well at all?"

"Surprisingly," Zamora says. "My arm was hurting like hell and then it just calmed down."

At least I fed the good dog something yesterday, Danny thinks, his eyes quickly scanning the surroundings for any sign that La Loca's body has been found in the night.

"No trace of her," Darko says, reading Danny's thoughts. "I was up again at five, double-checking under the crane. No police or reporters sniffing around either."

It's as if the events of the past few days had no consequence. But that can't be right. Everything we do matters, Dad always said. It all spreads out from us, rippling away. *You just can't see that happening sometimes, Old Son.*

He knows full well that any lull can only be temporary.

"But how could she just disappear?" he groans. Somehow not being able to find the body makes the whole thing much worse. Creepier.

Darko rubs his chin. "No idea. Here, come with me a minute, will you?"

"Why?"

"I want to be certain we're looking in the right place."

Danny nods, pleased that Darko's taking the problem seriously. He lets the knife thrower lead him through the tangle of vehicles, up onto the huge flight of steps that run from the cathedral. It feels exposed out here in the sunshine and Danny glances around anxiously.

"Never taken a life before," Darko says. "To tell the truth, it was a lousy shot. I was aiming for her arm. Must have been the wind. Urrrghhh . . ."

"You didn't have a choice."

It's so unusual to see Darko looking like this, and Danny wants to help if he can. Again, he remembers the night of the failed water escape, seeing the knife thrower help a half-drowned Dad to the family trailer.

"Maybe not," Darko says.

He leads them down the stairs to where they have a good view of the entire building. "Which one do *you* think she fell from?"

Danny shades his eyes and peers up into the

bright morning. A few cumulus clouds are moving in off the sea, but otherwise, the sky is crisp, clear. The canary-colored cranes tower dizzyingly above the cathedral. *I was up there*, he thinks. *I nearly fell* . . . His knees feel watery at the thought, but he concentrates, studies the Sagrada, the scaffolding—then points resolutely.

"It was that one. I'm sure."

"That's what I thought." Darko shakes his head.

"The more we know, the less we know, right?"

His eyes seek out Danny's. "You *sure* you saw Jimmy that night?"

Danny nods. "But he couldn't be behind *all* this, could he?"

The knife thrower returns Danny's gaze for a long moment, then looks up into the sky. "He was always very private—intense. Something was dragging him down, unbalancing him."

Overhead, a big cloud is rolling over the city, purple undersides, towering white heights above. Darko jerks his unshaven chin at it.

"Know how much one of those weighs? If you compressed all the water inside, it would make something like a billion kilograms. Even the clouds are too heavy to stay up forever. Everything falls in the end, right? Clouds, people. Even the greatest wire-walkers, the Blondins and Wallendas of this world. And certainly people like Jimmy—"

Zamora hurries over toward them. "Danny! The boys tell me they saw a guy hanging around last night, spying on our encampment. And Tweedledum says they saw him again, just half an hour ago."

Darko looks sharply at the dwarf. "What did he look like?"

"Tall. Longish hair. Hurried away when they went to challenge him. Any ideas?"

"Well, it's not Jimmy. He's not much taller than you, Zamora."

Danny's gaze flicks out, through the bars, to where the tourists are lining up for entrance to the cathedral. Some of them are eyeing the unlikely trio, curiosity aroused. Beyond them—just for a moment—he thinks he sees a pair of eyes locked straight on him, a tractor beam of a gaze from some-one motionless in the jostle and movement of the square. But then the line shuffles forward, and there's just empty air beyond.

As he returns to the shelter of the vehicles, he sees Sing Sing emerging from Rosa's caravan. She flicks him that quick half smile, mutters a good morning, and then looks away again.

"Are you OK, Sing Sing?"

"Yep. Talked a bit with Rosa last night."

"And?"

"Not much. She was obviously crazy about Jimmy at one time. Who knows why!"

"I didn't know he was so keen on Mum—"

"Turns out we didn't know much about Mum, did we?" Sing Sing fires back, her voice brittle.

Danny opens his mouth, then hesitates. His first instinct is to defend Mum, but at the same time, he desperately doesn't want to drive a bigger wedge between him and Sing Sing. He wants—needs—her on his side.

"I'm sure when we know why . . ."

Sing Sing shrugs. "Look, forget it. I've got to find Darko. He's asked me to help him."

"What with?"

"He wants me to be his new target girl."

"Really?" Danny's eyes open wide. "Are you sure you want to do that? I heard he clipped Izzy last year—"

"Rosa said it's because she can't keep still. I'm a big girl, you know."

She sounds irritated by his concern and turns to

go, but Danny catches her arm. "We're still friends, aren't we?" he asks quickly.

"Blood's thicker than water, right?" Sing Sing smiles that defensive smile again, but there's just a little more warmth in it this time. "And circus blood is even thicker than that. Funny thing is, Darko says I'm a dead ringer for Lily!"

She pulls her arm free and turns toward Darko's camper van as the dark cloud rolls away overhead, dragging its shadow across the city.

For the rest of the day Danny keeps half an eye on the crowds milling beyond the railings—but the thoughts of Berlin are pressing now, filling his mind, and the time drags. *Just want to get going*, he thinks. He imagines walking the paths of the Tiergarten under the bare trees, seeing graffiti on remnants of the Berlin Wall, standing again in that regimented cemetery. What will it feel like, being back in those familiar places? Being at Mum and Dad's graveside? The journey—both desired and feared for so long—is just hours away, and he doesn't want to wait a second longer than necessary.

At last, as night falls across the cathedral's towers, showtime approaches and people start to take their seats for the performance.

The company members gather together in the wings, and Danny watches them stretching, putting chalk on their hands, patting one another on the back. That preshow atmosphere—the nerves, the concentration, the excitement—is so familiar, so precious that it softens his impatience for a moment.

The others break off their warm-up when they see Zamora returning from his hospital appointment. They all cluster around him, taking turns to sign the new cast on his arm.

The dwarf beckons Danny over. "There you are, *amigo*! I've saved a prime spot for you."

"What should I write?"

"Whatever you want, of course!"

Danny hesitates for a moment but then writes: *For my friend Zamora, the rock of the Mysterium. Danny.*

"Thanks, *amigo*." The Major smiles and squeezes Danny's shoulder. "Glad I've still got your confidence."

It's not quite the truth, but Danny nods. "Can I borrow your phone?"

"Sure. Why?"

"Mine's useless now. I want to get hold of Inspector Ricard before the show starts."

"Be quick then."

Sing Sing grabs the pen and squiggles four Chinese characters on the cast.

"And what does that say?" the strongman asks her, squinting at her message.

"Roughly translated: *'Practice makes perfect,'*" she says. And everyone laughs. Just for a moment—in that laughter—Danny feels the old camaraderie of the company flicker fully into life around him, uniting the group.

Beyond the curtain, the audience members talk excitedly.

"How long until curtain?" Danny asks Rosa.

"Five minutes. I've saved you and Zamora the best seats in the house."

He pulls away to one side and hurriedly dials Ricard's number, rehearsing in his mind what he needs to tell the detective.

A series of clicks, a crackle on the line, and he hears the inspector's phone ringing. Then the voicemail kicks in.

"This is Jules Ricard, please leave me a message and I'll get back to you."

It's good to hear the detective's measured voice but frustrating not to be able to speak directly. Danny leaves as precise a message as he can and then, as the houselights dim and an expectant hush settles on the audience, he slips through the curtain to take his seat next to Zamora.

"Any luck?" the Major whispers.

"Voicemail. I asked him to call back."

Zamora sighs. "Never thought I'd be saying this, but I'll be glad to get out of here."

"What about Javier's funeral?"

"Lope understands," the Major says, pulling a face.

"Poor Javier—his poor little kids . . ."

But then the thunderous intro music starts to build, the spotlights shine, and—despite everything—Danny feels that old thrill reaching up to snare his heart. Something glorious is coming. Something wonderful. Roll up! Roll up! Here comes the Mysterium . . .

The Klowns and Aerialisques fly through the rolling smoke, and Danny settles to watch—reveling not just in the spectacle but also in the knowledge that comes with being an insider. There's Frankie dressed in black, strapping himself into a harness, ready to counterweight Maria on her solo straps routine. The spotlight is on the Australian aerialist, but the rigger's supple work, his controlled drop that propels Maria high into the air, is just as thrilling. Danny finds himself sitting on the edge of his seat, his heart up in his mouth. It still feels like magic, even though he's seen it a thousand times before.

A smile slides across his face and lingers there.

But as the first half finishes, Darko comes pushing through the crowds, his face stormy.

"We just saw that guy again! He was *inside* the compound, near my camper. And my wallet's gone—and my bloody passport with it!"

The spell cast by the show is broken in a moment. Danny jumps to his feet. "Get the others, Major."

"I'm coming with you," Zamora growls.

They hurry from the performance space to find the Tweedle brothers waiting on the south steps of the cathedral, their eyes straining to pierce the gloom, the ink-pool shadows.

"He was near the big truck," Tweedledee says, "but then I lost him."

"The same man?" Darko asks. "Tall, you say?"

The man nods his curly head. "Taller than you. Skinny."

There's a movement away to the left, in the black space between Rosa's caravan and the cathedral wall, someone hugging the shadows. But as the figure eases away his face shows pale for a second in a streetlight.

Danny sees him first—and is off and running before anyone else has time to react. He hurls himself down the lower steps, three at a time; plants a foot on a low wall; and vaults clear over the Mysterium's humming generator. Watching the show has put fresh belief and energy back into his system. Now, adrenaline pumping, he attacks the shadows where he saw the figure.

Just too late—gone. But there are footsteps hurrying away into the night. Danny heads after them, round the side of the cathedral—and finds a dead end. The man is trapped, his long, angular frame caught for a moment, indecisive as he looks right and left. The Sagrada's high pointed railings run straight into the wall of the building itself. *He's cornered*, Danny thinks. *His only way out is back past me—maybe he'll turn and attack. I'd better wait for Darko and the others.*

But the man—his long dark hair twitching as he moves—has another plan. He grabs the railings and climbs fast, his jacket flapping as he scrabbles to the top of the ten-foot-high fence, more determination than technique in his movements. And then, in a tangle of legs and arms, he flips over the spikes and drops to the ground. His landing is awkward and he stumbles, hands bracing on the pavement.

Danny's already climbing, trying to catch a better glimpse of the man. But he's on his feet again, and—without glancing back—he dashes away through the mopeds and cars to a chorus of horns. Within seconds he's disappearing into the thick shadows of the park beyond.

The railings are harder to climb than they look. Danny loses his grip. His feet slip—once, twice. By the time he's reached the top and is trying to work out how to get over the spikes, there's no sign of the man. At least they're much less sharp than they appear from the ground. Maybe the man knew that and planned his escape? Danny negotiates his way over them, shimmies to the ground, and then slips across the road as the traffic lulls.

He slows to a brisk walk as he passes the shuttered kiosks, parked motorbikes and cars.

"Wait for me, Danny," Darko shouts from the top of the railings. "I'm right behind you!"

But there's no time to wait. *The man will be gone if I'm not quick*, Danny thinks. He hurries forward and enters the hush under the darkened trees.

There's dense foliage on all sides. It would be easy to hide in there but hard to move quietly through it. He stops and listens intently, but there's nothing to hear. Farther down the long path, a few homeless people are camped out on the benches, cocooned in cardboard and old blankets.

Danny trots on, swiveling his head side to side, ears pricked, passing the sleeping forms of the homeless on their hard beds, newspapers pulled over their faces. The man's more than likely already out the far side of the park—but you never know. Ahead, there's a group of men perched on one bench. They look seedy, rather desperate, shoulders hunched hard up to their ears, trying to gain a bit of happiness from the bottle they're passing from hand to hand. Danny quickens his pace—but one of the men breaks into a broad smile, teeth white in the gloom.

"Bona tarda, Señor!" he shouts and then points meaningfully, urgently, back at one of the benches Danny's already passed. There's a seemingly comatose body laid out there under a mess of newspapers and cardboard. *"El hombre esta ahi!"*

He jabs his finger for emphasis. Danny stops, turns, takes a few steps back—and, as he does so, the figure on that bench throws the newspaper from his face and leaps to his feet.

It's the dark-haired man. He glances at Danny, seems torn for a second between attacking and fleeing, but then he sees Darko hurrying into the park—and darts away into the undergrowth.

"After him!" the knife thrower shouts.

Twigs and branches and thorns snag at Danny as he gives chase, his feet treading hard earth. Darko is crashing his own way through the bushes off to his right, and they're closing in on their target—there's a brief glimpse of the man's angular body knifing through the foliage ahead.

But seconds later, he's free of the tangle. Through the branches Danny watches the man hurdle a low gate and run to a parked motorbike. He kicks it off its stand and guns the engine in a running start. As Danny emerges from the undergrowth, there's a roar, and the figure in the dark suit is powering out into the traffic, slaloming around yellow taxis.

"Can you make out the registration number?" Darko calls.

But the lights are dim, and as the bike pulls away,

all Danny is able to see is the letter *M* and the numbers 3 and 5. The rider powers into a right-hand corner, jumps a red light—correcting hard to avoid a bus—and is gone.

Across the street the intro music for Act Two of the show is already building deep within the Sagrada: thunderous drums audible over the hum of traffic.

Danny looks up at the knife thrower. "We're not safe yet, are we?"

Darko takes a deep breath. "Not by a long shot. Good thing we're on our way tomorrow. I've got to get onstage—and then go and report the theft."

But the rest of the show passes without incident.

In fact, it's better than that. Despite all the distraction and problems facing the company, it's a triumph. The audience stands and cheers and stamps the floor, calling the company back for three curtain calls.

Rosa looks like she's regained self-belief as she strides out of the spotlight, Cyr wheel in hand, breathing hard, her tattoos glistening. She gives Danny a big hug.

"You see?" she beams. "We've still got it, *Bello*." Danny waits until she's released him and then breaks the news to her about the intruder.

Rosa groans. "*Mamma mia.* If we could just have one show without interruption or worry! That's all I ask."

"I suggest we get going tonight," Zamora says. "Drive through the early hours."

Sing Sing has come over to join them, her own face still glowing from what she's just seen.

Rosa nods. "Why not? We'll get a clear run out of the city and put everything here behind us. We'll be in Naudy by midmorning."

"Naudy?" Danny stumbles, wrong-footed. "I thought it was Berlin next."

"We've got to collect the big tent," Rosa says, "and some other equipment. It's en route. We'll have a couple of days there to regroup—"

"What's Naudy for flip's sake?" Sing Sing says.

"Winter quarters," Rosa says. "A big house in France, in the countryside. It belongs to Izzy and Bea's family, and we've got workshops there and a practice space in the barn . . . It's amazing, right, Danny?"

Danny nods. At least it always used to be. Right

now, he just wants to be going—to get to Berlin—and the thought of a delay is frustrating.

"So why's everyone looking so worried?" Sing Sing presses. "Danny? Did I miss something?"

"Seems we're not in the clear yet."

"Of course not, dummy," she says with a smile. And this time it holds for a moment, as if the show itself has worked some kind of release on her too. "But we'll be OK."

"How do you know?"

"Our luck's turning—look what I found."

She reaches under her long black hair and pulls something from around her neck: it's Dad's lockpick set, glinting in the light.

"Just looked down and there it was."

The find lifts Danny's mood as he helps the others roll flight cases into the trailer. Maybe the intruder was no more than an opportunistic thief after all—nothing to do with Danny. *He'd have realized that we're in and out of the vehicles all the time and that stuff wouldn't be locked. And at least, I don't have much to lose—*

But what about Sing Sing's birth certificate? The book from Dad—and that last message on the envelope? Danny rushes over to his rucksack, hands working fast. Still all there!

The Klowns are coming up the ramp, dragging the rolled safety net. Bjorn passes him and flashes a smile his way.

"Almost like you're one of the gang again, Danny," the big man says. "You can take the boy out of the circus, but you can't take the circus out of the boy. Am I right?"

"Faster!" Rosa shouts. "Don't just stand there, Danny. Pack your stuff."

"Sorry, Rosa," he mumbles, forgetting for a moment that *he's* the one who's meant to be cross with *her*. Hurriedly he rolls up his sleeping bag.

And the tightly folded note that's been slipped inside it flutters to the floor like a dying butterfly—and it, with the threat it carries, is trampled underfoot, and lost.

5

WHEN YOU PUT YOUR FOOT IN IT

An hour and a half later, under bright Catalan stars, the Mysterium convoy rolls out of town and onto a near-deserted motorway. Danny lets out a long breath of relief. At last they're on the road!

They've left behind the Sagrada, the lights of Tibidabo on the hills above the city, the shuttered and silent Park Güell. Ahead you can make out the Pyrenees, their forms cutting jagged against the night sky. And waiting somewhere over the dark horizon is Berlin.

Danny's sitting up high in the cab of the prop trailer, with Sing Sing beside him, her head lolling in sleep against his shoulder. Next to her, Rosa is gripping the steering wheel and pressing the accelerator to the floor, staring down the night.

"Good to be moving again, isn't it, *Bello*?" she shouts over the engine. "I get jumpy if I'm anywhere for more than a few days." She smiles. "Runs in my family. We Vegas have always been wanderers."

And, despite the fact that he's still annoyed with her, he knows she's right.

Even with keeping his eyes wide and watching for trouble, even with the impatience to get going, Danny's almost—*almost*—managed to enjoy the last hour or so: the last check to make sure all the equipment is stowed, the engines warming up, the excitement of embarking for a new destination, taking your world with you.

As they slipped through Barcelona at one in the morning, he could imagine himself back in the days before the tragedy, riding at the head of the convoy, glancing in the mirror to see the rest of the vehicles dancing round a corner behind them: Darko's purring red camper, the van with the Klowns towing the generator, the minibus, and cars and caravans bringing the rest of the crew. This evening as they left the city, their reflection slipping across shop windows, he caught glimpses of the glowing word on the trailer's side—*MYSTERIUM*—reversed off the darkened glass, and felt a kind of brief elation. A sliver of hope between the dark thoughts.

The special camaraderie of the road again! *Yes, I do belong here,* he thought. *I felt that when we were laughing with Zamora, when I was watching the show. And definitely now. Whether it's with the Mysterium or another company, this is what I know and love. This is the life I want . . .*

The decision felt good, putting fresh strength into his body—but then grief clouded it.

Now, of course, there was one vital piece of the convoy missing: his own family trailer thumping along behind the 4×4, with Mum at the wheel and Dad scribbling notes, alterations to the show, before they'd even left the city's limits. That's when Mum and Dad were at their most alive, eyes already trained on the horizon, eager for a new city, a new day.

Danny leaned his forehead against the juddering glass, watching the reflections of the convoy whip in and out of existence.

"Get some sleep, *Bello!*" Rosa calls now, taking a sip from her insulated coffee mug.

He shakes his head, thoughts of their destination burning their way to the surface again. "What exactly's going to happen in Berlin?"

"What do you mean?"

"Are we going to be . . . in the same place as before?"

Rosa sighs. "Pretty much. Near the Tipi Zelt, that cabaret venue in the park. Remember we climbed the monument in the snow? It was the day before—" She clicks her tongue, checking herself. "Listen, are you sure you're up to this, Danny? We could still—"

"I'm fine," he says crisply. "I want to go to the cemetery. To the graves."

"Of course, *Bello*. We'll all go when we've got a moment."

"I want to go as soon as we get there."

"As soon as we can, Danny. There's a lot to do for the setup. You know that." Rosa rolls her head, loosening her neck and shoulders. "Mind if I play some music?" Without waiting for an answer she slips an ancient cassette into the slot. A guitar starts to pulse the rattly speakers. "Old tech is the best tech, right? We always used to play this on the way back to Naudy!" She presses her foot down, feeding fuel to the engine. "Good times there, huh?"

Yes, good times, Danny thinks. Despite that undeniable desire to get to Berlin as quickly as possible,

54

the memories of Naudy are stirring: the road that climbed the hill, the trees all around—like you were a submarine rising out of green seas—and you were suddenly on the ridge, above the chestnut woods, driving up the dead-end road, into the driveway and "home" again. The grand old house itself had seen better days: shutters blistered and hanging by one hinge, water dripping into buckets when the thunderstorms crackled overhead. In summer you threw open all the windows and French doors and there wasn't much difference between inside and out. In the meadow behind the house, Mum rigged her main walk-wire and practiced for hours every day over the waving long grass and wildflowers. The swallows flashed blue around her head, and Dad would watch her proudly and say she was a swallow herself . . .

"Hey, Woo! Are you listening to me?" Sing Sing has woken up and is jabbing him in the ribs.

"Sorry."

"I said, do you think I can do the target girl thing?"

Danny looks at her, surprised—but pleased in a way—to hear her needing reassurance. "You've got nerves of steel, Sing Sing. Like Bird Millman!"

"Bet I shake like a jelly. Anyway, my heroes are the high-wire merchants: Petit, Maria Spelterini."

"You should've seen Mum," Danny says, without thinking.

Sing Sing frowns darkly. "Yes, I should've," she hisses. "But I didn't. Full flipping stop."

Danny winces and starts to reply, but Sing Sing turns to Rosa, raising her voice. "How long till we get there, boss?"

"Hours yet. How's everyone doing, Danny? All there?"

Cursing himself for being so thoughtless, he glances in the side mirror and counts the headlights of the convoy strung out on the otherwise deserted motorway. Immediately behind Rosa's trailer he can see Darko's face concentrating on the road, Maria next to him. Then the Klowns, the minibus. And Billy's old estate car. Frankie's rigging van is bringing up the rear, and the motorway lies dark behind.

"Yep—all there."

Danny's about to turn around again when he sees a light burning up behind the convoy, fast. Its single beam closes on them quickly—but then settles in behind the rigging van instead of passing. Danny watches it idly for a minute or so, wondering why it doesn't overtake the Mysterium vehicles. Wouldn't be the first time they've been followed, after all! It couldn't possibly be the guy from earlier that evening, could it?

Seems unlikely—but he keeps his eyes on it, trying to see the figure hunched behind the powerful beam. Suddenly the bike pulls out, headlight shaking as it bumps over the dotted lines, and roars past the convoy, engine opening up as if on a racetrack, its rider bent low, staring ahead. He doesn't cast as much as a glance at them.

As it flashes past, Danny's eyes instinctively seek out the license plate. German. B WS 2912. *Day before my birthday*, he thinks, *29 December*. Well, file it away, just in case. No *M* or 5 or 3 amongst the figures. He eases back in his seat. *Not everyone and everything is out to get you, dummy. Even though it feels like it. Got to keep rational now.*

The taillight fades fast into the darkness ahead and is gone.

"Get some sleep, kids," Rosa says again, yawning, and turns the music up another notch, so the speakers rattle even harder.

In the early hours they stop at a rest area just over the Franco-Spanish border. Ahead, the weather looks charged, gray. The air feels distinctly nippy. Away to the west, farther into the Pyrenees, snow is brightening the tops of the mountains.

Danny hops down from the cab, casting a wary eye across the parking lot. Things have felt uncomfortable again ever since he put his foot in it about "seeing Mum," and he's glad of the space, the fresh air. One by one, the others join him in the half-light.

Zamora shuffles up from the rigging van. "OK, Danny?"

"Think I upset Sing Sing."

"Then you'd better make it right. She spent most of the afternoon looking for your lockpick set, you know. Want anything to eat?"

Danny shakes his head. "I'm fine." He looks to see if Sing Sing needs anything, but she's still sitting up in the cab, staring ahead into the heavy clouds.

He watches the others stroll across the parking lot and then clambers back up into the cab, pulling the door shut with a clunk.

"Thanks for finding the lockpick set."

She nods. "Talk about a needle in a flipping haystack!"

"I'm sorry about earlier. I didn't mean to upset you."

"No," Sing Sing says quietly. "I'm sorry *I* snapped. I guess I'm struggling a bit . . ." She sighs out, long and hard, and then buries her face in her hands, muffling her voice. "What I want to say is I'm jealous, really. How come you got to live with your parents, to know them—even if it was all cut short—and I never got to even meet either of mine?"

"I'm sure Mum never meant to—"

"It's just *so* unfair. So bloody not fair." She thumps the dashboard for emphasis, then looks up, struggling to contain the ragged emotion that's bubbling up inside her. "I need to know why. Simple as that. The first thing I felt when we found the certificate was relief—excitement that I had you, that I had a half brother, family!—but now it's just a mess in my head."

Danny nods.

There's silence. An awkward silence broken only by the metallic clicking as the engine cools. He wants to say something but can't find the words to bridge the gap.

And now there are hurried footsteps outside, and Danny looks up to see Zamora virtually sprinting across the parking lot. With his good arm he's waving his phone in the air.

"Danny! It's Ricard!"

Danny jumps down and grabs the phone. "Hello? Monsieur Ricard?"

When the Interpol agent comes on the line, his voice is clipped, more rushed than Danny remembers. "Danny. I am so glad to catch you."

Where to start? The words tumble out: "Monsieur Ricard, there was a hit woman in Barcelona. She tried to get me, but . . . but I'm OK."

"I've heard some of it from contacts in Spain," Ricard says. "But I'm more worried about what's coming toward you next. We're getting good information from our informer about what the Forty-Nine are planning. Not a complete picture yet, though. Each part of the organization only has fragments of that—and no one has the whole image. Apart from Center, of course."

"Why does he want to kill me?" Danny blurts out and curses himself for sounding so weak, so desperate. But it's hard not to. That's the question that's been bounding against the inside of his skull ever since Javier's revelations.

"I'm still not sure, Danny. But it seems you have

something he wants. And . . ." The Interpol man hesitates. "And we need to be careful because there may be other parties involved. Not just Interpol . . ."

Danny stares at the distant mountains. "What do you mean? This is something to do with Dad, isn't it?"

"Harry was in what we call 'deep cover.' We didn't know what he was working on for a year or more at a time, Danny. He was on his way to see me—said he had something vital—and then the fire took him and your mother. Seems, regrettably, that our communications were being monitored—"

The line stutters, goes dead, but then Ricard's voice comes again. "Danny, I'm in a dash for a plane now. Rome. But we're pretty sure the Forty-Nine are planning a major crime—and it looks like it's happening in Germany. We've identified a few section heads, and they're all heading that way now. Could well be Berlin. I'll be on a plane for there in three days—"

Could be a coincidence, Danny thinks. *But it may mean the Forty-Nine are still one step ahead of me.* The breath tightens in his chest. "Monsieur Ricard, what about my aunt Laura? Is she OK?"

The line goes down again—for a good ten seconds—before Ricard's voice comes back in broken pieces. ". . . trial judge . . . she'll be . . . good chance . . . the main thing is to watch out for . . . hello? . . . tunnel . . . you hear me, Dan—"

And now nothing but dead air. When Danny tries the number again, he just gets a Cantonese voice rattling off an automated message.

Sing Sing is leaning out of the window. "Well?"

"I'll tell you in a minute. I need to get something to drink. Can I get you anything?"

"No, thanks. Brother." She says the last word cautiously, making air quotes with her fingers, then flicks her eyebrows into that arch shape again. *She doesn't seem convinced*, Danny thinks, *but I like the sound of it. I wonder when—if—I should call her "sister" again?*

Preoccupied with that thought and with what Ricard had to say, Danny grabs an Orangina in the shop and lines up to pay.

The sleepy cashier is fiddling with a jammed till roll and swearing under his breath in French. Across the parking lot the company members are piling back into the convoy, the Mysterium letters shining in the gloom, Frankie tightening straps on the scaffold lashed to the rigging van. Other vehicles are pulling in—and as people climb out of their cars, they all glance curiously at the traveling circus. Adult or child, the sight snags their attention for a moment. How often after a show has Danny heard people say: "Wow, makes me want to dye my hair and tattoo my arms and run away with you lot." It confirms that decision made out on the motorway. *Circus till I die*, he thinks.

But then his attention is snared by something closer. Just on the other side of the plate glass windows, there's a row of parked motorbikes. And sitting on one of them is a familiar-looking figure. He has his back to Danny, but instantly brings to mind the man they chased in the darkened Sagrada park. The same angular tension and slight stoop in his body, same dark hair—and his focus, despite the unfolded map on his knees, seems angled toward the Mysterium vehicles beyond. Could it be the same guy? Danny hadn't really noticed the bike that the thief took, and anyway this license plate is a German one. B WS 2912. *That's strange—it's the same one that swished past on the motorway last night. Surely he'd have been hours ahead of us by now?*

And it *does* look like the thief, Danny thinks, moving to get a better view. As the first rays of sunlight slide across the forecourt, the rider grabs a black helmet and jams it over his head. He glances round, eyes shielded behind old-fashioned motor-bike goggles, then kicks the engine into life and rolls forward, his boots out, skimming the tarmac as he cruises away from the service building, toward the convoy.

Danny runs through the sliding doors and out of the shop. The biker has paused just thirty or so paces from the prop trailer, engine idling, as he fiddles with something in the vehicle's storage compart-ment. Or pretends to? The pale light of dawn makes the scene unreal. The man straightens again and sud-denly guns the engine, carving away onto the exit road, engine snarling, accelerating hard.

A heavy hand clamps Danny's left shoulder. "Young man! *Vous n'avez pas payé pour ça!*"

Danny looks at the forgotten drink clutched in his hands, then back up to see the helmeted rider vanish behind the glowing red sign of the gas station.

6

WHEN SOME THINGS STAY THE SAME

The miles roll past under thickening skies. Cold rain spots the trailer's windscreen, and the wipers shudder into life, leaving blurry streaks.

"*Mamma mia*," Rosa growls. "The weather doesn't look that good ahead. And it's not even December yet!"

She squints through the windscreen, stamina developed by years and years of life on the road, guiding the convoy up the long drags and drops of southwestern France, as place-names familiar from old tours slip past: PERPIGNAN, TOULOUSE, MONTAUBAN. For an hour or so Danny has kept up a tense vigil for the man on the motorbike, but there's not a trace of him. *Maybe I was mistaken*, he thinks. But if it *was* him, then he must be more than a common thief. He must be a spy for the Forty-Nine.

Eventually, with no further sighting of the man, he gives up and pulls Dad's Proust book from his backpack. Might as well make good use of the time.

Why was it in the cache in the Güell? He flips through the pages. Maybe there are marks picking out particular words? Or even something tiny wedged in a fold of the paper? After thirty minutes of searching, he has to accept there's nothing. *Maybe Dad just wanted me to read it one day,* Danny thinks dejectedly. Wouldn't be that unusual—even for something like this. *He likes to teach people,* Laura always said. *Even when they don't want to be taught!*

He tries to concentrate on the first few pages, but the prose is dense, tricky going, and the book shakes in his hands, so he puts the book to one side, thinking of Laura. In the rush of events that overtook them in Barcelona, he's hardly had time to worry about his aunt. She will be coping, he has no doubt. She's faced worse. And those ridiculous charges—presumably cooked up by corrupt officials in the pay of the Mafia or the Forty-Nine—will probably be laughed out of court when the trial happens.

But when will that be? How long will she be out of action? And what if—somehow—the charges do stick and she goes to prison? Would Zamora become Danny's guardian? Would he have to go back to boarding school in England?

Sing Sing waves a hand in front of his face. "Danny? Anyone home?"

"Yep. I was just thinking about Laura."

"She'll be OK. Fancy playing cards?"

He doesn't really—just wants to keep that watchful eye on the highway or pick away at the code—but he's glad Sing Sing's reaching out to him again. "OK, sure."

She takes the pack and starts to shuffle. "No cheating, right, Danny?"

"Wouldn't do that—to my half sister," he says. Sing Sing hesitates—a smile forming at the corner of her mouth—then starts to deal out the cards.

———————

It's already twilight as they pull past Fumel and start the climb out of the valley toward Naudy. The trailer's engine is rough as they struggle up the steep hill, gears grinding, past the familiar landmarks of the timber yard, the church, the Café des Sports with its ancient, grubby yellow canopy. *Everything changes and nothing changes*, Danny thinks. *People come and go— people die—but café awnings stay the same.*

Outside, the darkness is thickening and birds are flying into roost, and he scours each shadow now for a hint of someone lying in wait. A hunter returning to a beat-up Peugeot, shotgun rested on shoulder, makes Danny's heart beat faster.

They round the last three tight, steep corners and emerge onto the ridge, lifted high above the valley. The spring meadow is long gone, grass cut short, pale in the winter dusk. In his memory he's been seeing Naudy in the summer, but now he remembers what winters were like. No central heating, drafts, damp. You could find ice skinning the inside of the bedroom windows or mice nesting in your duvet, and everyone huddled close to the big fire in the old ballroom. Candles lit everywhere to lift the gloom. The place felt mysterious and creepy and thrilling all at once . . .

Low clouds are smudging the skyline as they bump up the unpaved track, past the ghost houses of the holiday rentals, through the stone gates, and onto the weed-strewn drive.

A roughly hand-painted sign says *Bienvenue au Château Mysterium*. Its white letters and blue-black background are weathered and peeling. Sing Sing is peering at the building's two and a half stories, brooding and dark in the twilight, the shutters closed on some windows and all the others black.

She pulls a face. "Some flipping chateau!"

But Rosa's frowning too, pointing at the top row of windows. The last one at the far end of the building is emitting dim light.

"Someone left a lamp on," she groans. "No one thinks about the bills but me."

"Are you expecting anyone?" Sing Sing asks.

"No," Rosa says. "Just us."

"Maybe it was the housekeeper," Danny says, but his senses have already kicked right back into alert mode. Quickly, he scans the rest of the building, the deep shadows around the corner of the house. *Maybe the Forty-Nine know we're coming*, he thinks. *Maybe that biker really was the man from the park and he's beaten us here. Can't take any chances. Even Naudy might not be safe now.*

"Doubt it was Madame Dubois, Danny," says Rosa. "She's even stingier than me!"

Sing Sing puts her hand on Danny's arm. That

same charged touch she used to alert him when they were fighting the triads back in Hong Kong—the one that says, get ready for trouble.

"Doesn't matter who left it on. Someone just switched it off!"

7

WHEN ANTIQUES ARE DANGEROUS

A quick council of war convenes in front of the darkened house.

"Any of your family meant to be here?" Danny asks Bea.

"Not since the spring."

"I'll get the key," Izzy says and goes to the old flowerpot under one of the shutters on the ground floor. She rummages around, and then curses and looks back at them. "It's gone. Someone must have let themselves in."

Sing Sing's still staring at the now darkened window. "I think I saw movement. What's that room?"

"Just one of the bedrooms—we never use that end of the house much," Rosa says.

Zamora's rattling the door handle. "Locked. Can you do it, Danny?"

"No. Those old locks are too deep—the pick won't reach."

"Then we'll go in the back," Darko says. "The kitchen door's still got the special security method, hasn't it?"

"What's that?" Sing Sing asks, the whites of her eyes bright in the gloom. Darko makes it sound like a fancy time lock or combination.

"Plank propping it shut from inside," Danny says.

"Typical Mysterium," Rosa adds. "It's all front!" They leave Bjorn and Frankie guarding the driveway and make their way round to the back, Herzog sniffing the ground hard, as if he's picked up a scent.

"Probably just those evil squirrels," Darko says. But the dog is racing ahead of them now, round the corner of the house, and instead of chasing off into the woods like normal, he bounds resolutely up the three stone steps to the back door.

"Allow me," Joey says, cutting ahead. "I'm good at it."

He grips the door handle and then rapidly, rhythmically vibrates the door in its frame.

"Quiet as you can," Darko hisses from behind.

"Doing my best," Joey grunts, as the door hammers away like thunder. Suddenly it gives, and he tumbles forward, sending the plank crashing to the tiled floor inside.

"Now they know where we are," Rosa groans. "No point creeping around. Let's go for it. Split up in groups of two or three—Joey, stay on this door."

"And for heaven's sake, be careful," Zamora adds. "Come on, you two. I want you with me. We'll take the ballroom and the dining room. Then the backstairs."

Beyond the kitchen, a long corridor stretches ahead into blackness. Zamora flicks the light switch, and a chain of dusty chandeliers illuminate the yellow walls with the company's collection of framed show posters and publicity photos. Danny's eyes rest briefly on an image of Dad, like the one he keeps at school—that old retro poster with the burning rope. Frozen in time behind the glass, nothing changed, except now he—Danny—has done that trick! Or at least his own version of it. For a second his eyes are locked on Dad's. *Talk to me*, he thinks. *Tell me what that last clue is all about.*

He can hear the others fanning out. Voices calling to one another in distant parts of the house.

"Come on! I'm up for a fight," Sing Sing says, her hands ready, cocked martial arts style.

"Hopefully it won't come to that," Zamora says. "Let's take the ballroom next."

The far end of the corridor opens into a big high-ceilinged room. One by one, the lights on the walls flicker into life, revealing faded grandeur: mirrors fogged with age, scrolling, chipped plaster-work, ancestral portraits. Piled to one side is a mess of equipment: collapsed trapeze rigs, teeter boards, crash mats, unicycles, flight cases. Half-open wardrobes spill costumes out across the wooden floor.

"Man, you *have* been burgled," Sing Sing whispers.

Danny shakes his head. "It always looks like this." He leads the way into the next room.

There's more order in here. White dust cloths cover a massive table and twenty or so chairs—big enough to seat the entire company and more. A menagerie of stuffed animals gaze down from the shelves above: perplexed, snow-white barn owls, startled yellowing stoats, a badger raised on its haunches, its glassy eyes blindly reflecting the light. A collection of ancient weapons—dusty halberds, swords, hunting knives—is mounted on the walls.

"This place gives me the creeps," Sing Sing says quietly.

"It'll grow on you," Zamora says. "Let's take the backstairs." He peers up the darkened flight and flicks a switch but nothing happens. "Bulb's gone. The wiring here's always been dodgy."

But Danny's spotted something. Amidst the collection of antique blades and guns, there's a darker patch on the fading wallpaper. A large, curved knife of some kind is missing. Whoever is lurking in the chateau must be armed!

Without waiting for the others, Danny surges up the stairs, keeping one hand on the wall as he waits for his eyes to adjust to the dark. Sing Sing bounds up behind him, her presence at his shoulder reassuring.

"Wait, you two," Zamora puffs. "I'm injured, remember."

"I've got to warn the others," Danny shouts, reaching the top and turning right along the first floor corridor, past the landing of the main staircase.

He runs the length of the hall, around the corner into the neglected end of the building, as lights flicker into life behind him.

"Rosa!"

The ringmistress has just reached the room at the very end of the corridor. She disappears inside, and Danny rushes after her, banging through the door.

The room is empty—but distinctly warmer than the rest of the house. Rosa stands there—a puzzled expression on her face, hands on hips, looking at a small electric heater that's only just been switched off. A dull orange still glows in the heating element. Nearby, a dilapidated armchair has been turned to face the black rectangle of the window. On the bed is a rolled sleeping bag—and there's an ashtray on the windowsill, filled with half-smoked butts. The taste of smoke is in the air. Rosa picks one up, looks at it, and frowns.

"Were you calling me, Danny?"

"Yes. I think they've got a knife. There's one missing from the dining room."

"Maybe it's just theft after all, then," Rosa says, as Sing Sing arrives breathless in the doorway.

Danny shakes his head and goes to sit in the sagging armchair. "They were keeping watch. Look." The view from here is a commanding one of the driveway as it snakes through the trees toward the distant road. In the foreground, you can see Bjorn and Frankie, their bald heads reflecting light from the house. "This is the best room for it. You could watch the driveway, the road in—and headlights coming along the ridge."

"Whoever it was," Rosa says, sniffing the stale air suspiciously, "they've either jumped out of a window or slipped by us."

"Or are still hiding," Danny says. "They must have been watching the approach for a reason. They can't have gone far."

At least it only looks like one person, he thinks, *not a whole gang of criminals. Together we should be a match for whoever it is.*

But a painstaking check of the entire chateau fails to reveal the intruder. From the rubbish-choked cellar, to the empty servants' rooms tucked under the eaves, there's no sign of the room's mystery occupant. No homeless person taking shelter, no knife-wielding maniac. Gradually, over the course of an hour, the tension subsides a degree or two, as each room is checked and given the all clear.

"Don't think there's anything else missing," Izzy

says, as they all gather back in the kitchen. "Can't be a robbery."

"And you don't make yourself at home when you're burgling, do you?" Joey says brightly. "You just get in and out. *Vite*."

It sounds like he's speaking from personal experience, Danny notes, remembering the rumors about the Klown's past.

Bjorn sticks his head in the doorway. "Just heard an engine. It started up at the back of the old barn and went down the cart track through the woods. No lights."

"A motorbike?" Danny asks.

"Maybe . . ."

Danny jogs back out onto the terrace and listens hard. Perhaps that's it, growling down the slope beyond the barn. Or maybe it's just a car on the valley road farther down.

"You'd have to know where the key was kept, if you were going to break in," Sing Sing says, coming up to join him.

"Anyone could spot that hiding place," Danny sighs, turning back toward the house. "We never used to worry about security much. Let's go and check that room again for clues."

Back in the bedroom, Sing Sing sniffs the stuffy air and pulls a face. "Who else would know we were here?"

"No one but the company really. Maybe that motorbike guy followed us—"

"How do you follow someone from in front of them, Danny?"

"Maybe someone's listening to what we're saying. On phones or something. Or worked out we'd be stopping here on the way to Berlin. You could find our winter quarters easily enough on the web."

"Or maybe it was just some tramp—"

She stops short.

From above their heads comes the sound of movement. A scrape and then a soft thud. Like something—a large bird or small animal—trying to be stealthy, but not quite managing it.

"What's up there?" she whispers.

"There's an attic, I think. But we've never used it."

It comes again, another scrape—and then a muffled sound that sounds distinctly like a sneeze.

"Don't suppose it could be a rat. A pigeon or something?" Sing Sing says uncertainly. The noise comes again, shifting over their heads, away from the front of the house.

Danny puts his finger to his lips, his gaze following the sound as it moves. He leads Sing Sing on tiptoe out of the bedroom, across the corridor, and into an identical but darkened bedroom on the other side. A chair is pulled from the mold-streaked wall, and above that, you can just make out a small hatch in the ceiling.

"Let's get Zamora," Sing Sing hisses.

But at that moment the Major comes thumping back down the corridor. "Where are you, Danny? Sing Sing?" he shouts. "I told you to stick with me!"

He shoves his head into the room and sees Danny already standing on the chair, his hands reaching for the hatch release.

"What're you doing up there?" Zamora says impatiently and bangs down the light switch. The bare bulb over their heads flashes, gives a sharp *clink*, and shatters—and the room, together with the corridor, and the whole house, is plunged into darkness. Danny catches his breath, his hands still touching the hatch. From overhead there's the sound of movement again, more urgent now. Coming toward him.

The Major curses, toggling the switch up and down. Beyond him the corridor is a deeper black.

"What's going on?" Rosa's voice comes echoing up the stairs.

"Fuses have blown!" Zamora calls. "You better get down off that chair, Danny."

"'But I think there's someone up here—"

The words are stopped short in his throat as the hatch suddenly jerks down, rattling violently in the dark, missing his head by a fraction. He reaches up to steady himself.

But he doesn't get a chance.

Two strong hands—thin, bony but very powerful—reach down and take hold of his upper arms, and yank him clear of the chair, dragging him up into the attic.

8

WHEN THERE'S A RAT
IN THE LOFT

The grip feels almost inhuman in its intensity.

The fingers are like iron, digging into his arm-pits, as Danny is dragged straight upward and banged through the opening. It happens so fast, there's no time even to register fear—just astonishment—and an instinctive fight for survival. He kicks hard, trying to wriggle free, or wedge himself in the hatch, but it's no use. The element of surprise and the strength of the grip mean he's lost the initiative.

His assailant pushes him roughly to one side, sending him sprawling across the gritty, cobweb-strewn boards, and he lands face-first in the grime. Behind him the hatch bangs shut. In the silence of the attic it sounds like a gun going off, and Danny flinches. A second later, he hears a bolt rattling home, locking him—and his unseen attacker—in the blackness.

He claws the sticky cobwebs from his face. From below there are muffled shouts—Zamora and Sing Sing calling his name—but then a voice rasps the air close to his head. Like one that hasn't spoken for days, weeks, months. A rusty hinge on a long disused door.

"Has *he* sent you?" it says, sharply. "Has he sent you? Tell him to leave me alone."

So familiar . . . but hard to place.

"Who are you?" Danny says. In the darkness his own voice sounds disembodied, weak. Put some diaphragm into it, Dad would say. *Make* them listen to you.

"Who *are* you?" he says again.

"Danny?" the voice says then. "Danny? Don't . . . don't make me hurt you!"

There's the whoosh of a match, the whiff of the sulfur. A flame dances in the air, and a gas lamp hisses into life, throwing a circle of white light that blooms, grows—and illuminates the deeply lined face of Jimmy Torrini.

The familiar hooded eyes are staring straight at him, blinking rapidly.

Danny's blood runs cold. All he can hear is a voice in his head—Dad's—rambling on about Daniel and the Lion's Den. *I'm in it now*, he thinks. *I'm looking at the lion.*

"One move and it's your last, boy."

"It's OK, Jimmy. I'm not going to do anything," he says, as calmly as he can, but his voice won't quite behave. It wavers, betraying him.

But it's clear now the man is at least as terrified as he is. His eyes radiate something stronger than anxiety, stronger than fear. They look wild—as if staring down the barrel of a gun—and skitter from Danny's face to the bolted hatch and back again. Something's come loose in Jimmy's head, you can see that, some vital piece of wiring. He looks as though he might be capable of anything . . .

His hair's disheveled, even crazier than before, a scrag of a beard on his defiantly raised chin, his jacket sleeves rolled up like he used to do for close-up magic. Only now does Danny see that his left hand is gripping the long and jagged hunting knife missing from the dining room wall downstairs. In the bright light Danny can make out the nicotine stains on Jimmy's fingers as they curl tightly around its handle.

"What are you doing here, shrimp?" the illusionist barks, his mood switching suddenly from wild panic to aggression. "Thought they'd packed you off to school. After Berlin." His eyes, dark, brooding, bore into Danny. "Has he sent you?"

"Has *who* sent me?" Danny asks again, genuinely puzzled, inching backward across the dirty floor, trying to give himself a little more space in which to react. His own fear is constricting his chest, and he's fighting to keep panic at bay—but the question makes no sense. *Need to keep Jimmy talking*, he thinks. *Try and reason with the man until the others open the hatch. Don't let emotions get out of hand, either his—or mine.*

But that's hard to do. Not only did Jimmy try to drown Dad, but—no matter what Rosa says—he may well have set the fire that night. He's dangerous and clearly not in full grip of himself. *Need a plan B,* Danny thinks, *just in case.*

His eyes flick away to the closed trapdoor. A heavy-duty steel bolt has been fitted on this side. Beyond that, the low-ceilinged attic runs away through the skeins of thick cobwebs into impenetrable shadow.

"The man who wants to kill me, of course!" Jimmy laughs, waving the knife around wildly. "I can't trust anyone now. Not even you, boy!"

Somewhere, deep down, Danny thinks, *he'll want to feel calmer. Maybe I can snag him with a quick hypnotic induction—offer him that chance to relax and let the tension go.* But the man's eyes are so bewildered, so slippery, it's going to be really hard to grab his full attention.

Jimmy jabs the knife back over his shoulder. "He's out there. I *saw* him!"

"What man?"

"The man in the middle of things. Come on, Danny, you were always a clever kid!"

There's a drumming now on the hatch. Zamora shouting. "Open up! Open up!"

"And maybe *you* want to hurt me, Danny," Jimmy says, his voice suddenly calm, quiet, considered. "After what I did to your dad."

Danny's heart ratchets up another beat. "What—what do you mean?"

"I plugged his stupid locks on the water torture. Put that big-head in his place, nearly drowned him. Lily was too good for him. It was me she loved, Danny. Me!"

He rams the tip of the knife into the boards beside him with a thunk. *Forget hypnosis,* Danny thinks, *maybe I should just take the initiative. Try and overpower him, then free the bolt . . .*

But the memory of those strong hands is still bruised into his upper arms. And after all, this is a chance—the chance to find out what he can, before the others break the hatch open. The secret's so close. If he can just keep calm enough.

Danny steadies his voice again. "Jimmy, I'm not going to hurt you. I absolutely promise."

The man looks at him, unblinking. Those recessed eyes burning black, resting for a moment on Danny's own. Maybe this is the chance? Danny brings his index finger up, trying to keep it steady, moving it slowly toward Jimmy's forehead, taking his vision with it . . .

"But I want you to relax. Relax. Then I'll help you. I promise. Whatever's happened, whatever's wrong, we'll sort it out, right? I just want to ask you something."

But how will I react, Danny thinks, *if Jimmy tells me he did set the fire, that he killed Mum and Dad? Then I'll be looking at my parents' killer . . .*

He loses focus and confidence for a moment, and the man's attention glances away.

"Pfff." Jimmy puffs the air impatiently through pursed lips. "You can't hypnotize Dr. Oblivion, idiot!"

"OK then. OK. Just tell me straight out. Why—WHY—did you set fire to our trailer?"

Jimmy recoils, his face puckering into deeper lines. "Fire? What are you talking about? I'd never hurt Lily."

"Maybe you were acting on orders. Did the Forty-Nine have you in their power? Did Center—"

There's a splintering from the hatch, and the bolt rips clear of the wood.

Jimmy screeches—like an owl striking at its prey—and lunges forward. The knife flashes, and Danny covers his head with his arms, warding off the blow that seems to be coming. But instead, Torrini brushes past him, catching him off balance and knocking him over. Danny rolls and turns to see Aki coming up through the hatch. Jimmy shrieks again—and then hurls the oil lamp at the Japanese flier. It shatters, throwing oil and flame around the opening. Aki retreats fast, covering his face.

"Arrrrgh!"

In the ragged, dancing light, Danny looks round to see Jimmy scurrying away through the cobwebs, retreating into the dark.

"It's Jimmy!" Danny shouts. "I'm going after him!" Without waiting for an answer, bent double under the rafters, he gives chase as fast as he can. *So close to the truth*, he thinks. *I'm not letting it go now. Jimmy was about to tell me something.*

In the flickering orange light he can just make out the former company member scuttling ahead—and then Jimmy disappears, faded into the blackness. The attic is low, the roof, bent by age, pressing down—and as the light dims to virtually nothing Danny has to feel his way forward, one hand reaching in front, the other just over his head feeling for low beams. Behind him, Aki—and now Darko—are both calling his name, but he hurries forward as best he can, body braced, eyes straining for any bit of light, for movement.

He glances back to see the flames licking the rafters around the hatch—his friends silhouetted, trying to smother the fire with a blanket—then turns and presses on into the cloying air, the webs, the dust of decades. Ahead, he can just hear the scuffling as Jimmy rushes forward.

"I just want to talk to you!" Danny shouts and simultaneously runs into a beam, taking a glancing blow to the head that sparks stars in his vision. He crouches down, losing valuable seconds, reaching up to rub the point of impact. Is that a vague light forward and to the right? A hole in the roof—or another way out? How far does the attic go? It feels much bigger than the house itself.

More cautiously, he moves forward again, hands braced in front, and suddenly blunts his fingers on rough brickwork. He can sense space opening up to the right. *Far end of the house*, he thinks. *That's the west wing.*

There's a sudden flurry of movement now, a frantic scratching, scraping, very close by. Jimmy's no more than a few paces away, his ghostly form perched on a box, working frantically to push up the tiles above his head. Danny crouches, then charges forward, both arms out ready to tackle Jimmy around the legs.

And then a horrible sensation.

He's ready to bring Jimmy down, prepared to dodge that jagged hunting knife, but not for the floorboards to feel soft beneath his feet, to give—and he's stumbling, sinking. There's a cracking sound underneath him, and then, without warning, he— along with a large chunk of ceiling—drops into the dark below.

It's no more than a second of falling, but it feels like ten times as much. He flails arms and legs to try a break-fall, hoping he isn't over the grand stairwell. Then—*whump*—he's hit something, landing awkwardly on his back in a mess of rotten floorboards and goodness knows what else, knocking all the air from his body.

Plaster and brick dust rain down onto his face, and somewhere over his head, far away, he hears hurried movement, fading quickly: Jimmy making his escape, taking all his fear and craziness and secrets with him.

And then there's silence.

9

WHEN ANTIQUES
ARE USEFUL

So agonizingly close.

Danny lies there for a moment, cursing the bad luck that made him—not Jimmy—cross the weak patch of the ceiling. *Just goes to prove Dad was wrong,* he thinks. *Sometimes we do make our luck, but sometimes we just tread in the wrong place.* He pulls the breath back into his body, checking that each limb is working properly, allowing his head to clear, for his heartbeat to come back down the gears.

Jimmy was out of control—that's clear enough. But what was all that stuff about "he's out there now"? He made it sound like one of those horror films that the Klowns like to watch late after a show, and the memory of the dread in Jimmy's eyes makes Danny shudder now. More confusingly, Jimmy seemed genuinely puzzled when challenged about the fire. There was a brief moment of clarity then, and he looked like the Jimmy of old. Normal—or at least whatever counted as normal for him, for the Mysterium.

Danny sits up and shakes his head, snorting the dust from his mouth and nose. It's still dark, but there's light flickering in the corridor.

Rosa's shouting. "What's going on? Danny? Are you there?"

And farther off he can hear Zamora bellowing "FIRE! Get an extinguisher!"

He looks up. Light zips across his face, blinding him for a second, and he hears Rosa's voice close beside him. "It's OK, Danny—you've had a very lucky landing."

The flashlight beam flicks away, and as he lifts himself up, he can feel the soft bounce of one of the antique beds under the wreckage. At least that's a piece of good luck—a soft landing! He's in one of the grander rooms at the "decent" end of the house. Izzy has joined Rosa now, her eyes swiveling up to the hole in the ceiling and back again to the bed.

"Louis XIV, Danny. Family heirloom. Nearly sold it last year when we needed the cash—"

"What *happened* to you?" Rosa interrupts.

"It was Jimmy. Jimmy Torrini!" Danny stutters, getting to his feet. "He was in the attic. He's got that big knife from downstairs—"

"Whoa. Slow down," Rosa says, helping him from the rubble.

"It was Jimmy. And he says someone's trying to kill him."

"You're kidding me!"

Danny shakes his head impatiently. "We have to find him—or this other man—quickly!"

Rosa wrinkles her nose, then snaps into action, striding back out into the corridor. "OK, everyone! Jimmy's in the house. Don't ask me how or why, but we need to find him. Frankie? Fix the fuses. Aki and Joey, get down here."

Danny joins her in the corridor and runs straight into Sing Sing.

"Thank God you're OK," she sighs, throwing her arms around him. "We could hear it all—and I was trying to follow you underneath . . ."

Danny shakes free of her grip. "We've got to find Jimmy—I think he went out through the roof or something. And we need to check the woods."

He grabs the flashlight from Rosa and sprints

down the grand staircase two steps at a time leaving Sing Sing trailing.

"Wait, dummy! You might need me!"

The front door has been unlocked and gapes wide to the night. Danny dashes out onto the graveled drive. There's the smell of smoke on the fresh, night air—and, distantly, you can hear shouts from upstairs where the fire is still being fought.

Bjorn is rooted in the middle of the driveway, gazing up at the roof. All at once the lights in the grand old house blaze back into life: almost every room lit and the windows shedding light out toward the woods, deepening the shadows.

"What's going on, Danny?" the big man rumbles. "Have you seen anyone come out—?"

But a voice cuts him short—Maria shouting from behind the house: "There's someone in the trees!"

Danny's already moving before she's finished. He sprints round the house, flashlight beam bouncing across the bushes and trees, to where Maria is standing stock still, peering into the night. She points.

"He was right there!" she says firmly. "A tall guy. Turned and ran for it when he knew I'd seen him."

Sing Sing has joined them, her eyes aflame. "Let's go then," she shouts. "Charge!"

She flies away across the grass, with Danny and Maria sprinting after her, through the blocks of light spilling from the house, to the edge of the scrubby oak woodland, the steep drop back into the valley.

About 150 feet below them, there's a light weaving in and out of the trees. Then, abruptly, it's extinguished.

"Is that Jimmy then?" Sing Sing hisses.

"Might be the other man he was talking about."

"Well, let's find out!"

They chase down the hill, stumbling on the sloping ground, dodging branches and bramble, running when they can. It's hard to see the footing, and roots and ivy snare their feet like trip wires. Every now and then Danny stops and sweeps his flashlight beam across the falling hillside, keen to pick up their quarry but worried too that it might make him an easy target for someone with a gun. He listens hard. There's a sharp crack below that makes him flinch— but no, it's just a branch snapping.

Maria joins him, breathing fast. "Was he armed?" he asks.

"Might have had a gun in his hand. Couldn't be sure."

Sing Sing goes crashing past, hurdling a tangle of

bush, pointing down and to the right. "I see him!" she shouts. "He's running that way across the hill."

And then there's a rumble as a motorbike engine coughs into life from somewhere just ahead of her.

"Stop! Stop—or we'll shoot," she screams, and leaps down a bank, dropping out of sight altogether.

There are a couple of dull thuds, a squeal from Sing Sing, then the sound of the bike accelerating fiercely. As Danny reaches the top of the bank, he sees its shadow slicing between the tree trunks. The headlight flares into life, and it's away, toward the valley below, jolting along the rutted farm track.

"Sing Sing?"

There's no answer.

Danny crashes down the tangled bank and lands on the track as the motorbike's red taillight curves away. It blinks behind the trees and is then snuffed out for good, leaving exhaust scenting the cold air.

His half sister is sitting on the near side of the track, leaning back on her hands, looking slightly dazed, shaking her head.

"What happened?"

"I cut him off," she says, breathing hard. "But he pretty much rode the bike straight at me. I jumped out of the way at the last second."

The engine's just a faint murmur now, way below. Danny kicks the ground, then turns and stares into the distance. Not quick enough!

"But something you might like to check out," she says, getting to her feet and pointing to a white square gleaming on the track a short distance away.

Danny walks over to it and looks down to see a license plate: B WS 2912.

So he was right to be suspicious of that guy at the service station! This must be the man making Jimmy so scared.

"I don't suppose there was anything under it? Did you manage to see?"

"Of course!" Sing Sing says proudly. "Spanish plate: 0354 CAM."

10

WHEN DWARVES
DREAM OF HEAVEN

Danny stalks back up to the chateau in silence. The same man still following the company, then. The one who stole Darko's passport. But if he's really a danger to them, why not have a go at them now? And why is he after Jimmy? For that matter, where *is* Jimmy?

The lights from the house are blazing out into the night, shimmering green through the ivy-enshrouded windows. A tang of smoke still hangs in the air, but there's no sign of it seeping out of the roof anymore. Danny's eyes sweep the bushes and outbuildings huddled around the main building, searching for any hint of movement, any sign of Jimmy lurking in the shadows. *Would Jimmy really have hurt me? He could have, but he chose to flee instead.*

He meets Rosa back in the hallway. "You had no idea Jimmy was here?" he says to her.

"God, no! I'm as surprised as you, *Bello*," Rosa says. She's either telling the truth—or doing a very good job of faking it. Cocking her head to one side, she adds, "Though I did wonder when I saw the half-smoked cigarettes. We've checked every room, scoured the attic—no trace of him in the house."

"What about the other buildings on the property?"

"The boys are searching them one by one now. *Mamma mia*, at least the fire's out."

Darko comes back across the driveway. "The barn's clear. I checked up in the hayloft too. Just in case. Joey and the girls are doing the cart shed, but my guess is he's long gone by now."

They all listen, but save for the distant sound of the twins calling to each other in French, the murmur of the wind in the branches, there's nothing to be heard.

Rosa turns to Danny. "And how about this other man down the hillside?"

"He's the same one I chased in the park."

Darko swears under his breath. "We should all keep together tonight—in the main room. Just to be on the safe side."

"I don't think we should stay," Danny says impatiently. "I think we should get going. Now!"

"We'll be fine for one night," Rosa says. "Besides, we've got to prep for Berlin. We've got to stay professional, Danny. Even with the world falling apart around us."

It takes a long time for the house to settle.

For once, all the vehicles are carefully locked and a lengthy double-check is made of every room. With nothing found, the company bolts itself inside for the evening. Fires are stoked in as many fireplaces as Billy and Frankie can manage, and bit by bit a semblance of warmth and calm returns. The Mysterium's members turn in one by one, snuggling down in sleeping bags in front of the main fire in the ballroom. Danny and Sing Sing take a sofa each, listening to the logs spit and hiss, and try to let the day's drama slip from their systems. After ten minutes or so, Sing Sing reaches out a hand and puts it on his shoulder for a moment.

"Try and sleep well."

"Thanks. You too."

Outside, he can hear owls hooting in the long, dark silence. A train in the distant valley. In his mind he finds himself rehearsing his visit to Mum and Dad in the cemetery, walking between the lines of graves, standing there looking at their names carved on a stone. Sleep thickens in Danny's eyes and he lets them close, half listening to Zamora and Darko and Rosa, who are gathered by the hearth, chatting softly.

"He must have lost his mind," Darko's saying. "Could be capable of anything."

"Poor Jimmy," Rosa says wistfully.

"Always knew he was fragile," Darko adds. "Remember how he used to go all twitchy when he did the Oblivion stuff. Used to freak me out!"

Zamora coughs, shifts on his seat trying to get his arm comfortable. "I wish we could have a word with him . . ."

"I expect he's long gone," Rosa says, then sighs. "Remember when we were all young and the world used to make sense?"

"No!" Darko laughs. "I don't!"

"I thought I knew everything," Rosa says. "Could do everything . . ."

Danny's dropping deeper. The gentle to and fro

of the chat reminds him of the camaraderie of the past again—the intense bond of a traveling company who must rely on one another for everything: food, companionship, safety . . . Maybe it can be rekindled properly, trust restored? Or maybe it's too late for that. At least for this incarnation of the Mysterium.

"Worst thing a performer could do, tamper with someone else's equipment. Might as well stick a knife in someone," Zamora grunts.

"It's over and done with," Rosa says. "And what I wouldn't give for some peace and quiet."

The Major adjusts his sling. "You should go to this spot I visited last year with Bjorn. It was on a little island in the middle of Lake Vänern—near his folks' place in Sweden. Near Karlstad. We rowed out to it on a super-still morning. There was mist hanging on the water. Not a sound but our oars—and when we got to the island, it was so silent. Pine trees and soft moss and dropped needles on the ground. And we sat there and said nothing and cooked fish on an open fire. Ahhh," he sighs. "That's what I'd like heaven to be. A quiet, peaceful island. Lapping water. And all the time in the world to watch a cloud drift across a blue sky. Isn't that right, Bjorn?" he adds, looking up as the catcher comes back in with more logs.

"That's right, man," Bjorn murmurs. "That was heaven that summer. But we're a long way from that. I just heard there's snow on the way in Berlin . . ."

. . . And in Danny's dream the snow is falling. Steady, insistent, thickening. He can hear crows crawking in the distance. And then see them: black smudges in the snowstorm flapping about. With a sinking feeling, he realizes he's back at school, in a language lesson, and he hasn't done his homework. The crows are busy in the trees, and there's a teacher he doesn't know standing at the whiteboard, reading from a textbook—but he's muttering in a strange, childish voice and it's hard to catch the words. Then, like a radio tuning to a pure, clear signal, he hears the teacher steadily counting: *fünf, zwo, acht, acht, vier—fünf, zwo, acht, acht, vier— drei, sieben, eins, eins, vier* . . .

For a moment, confused, Danny wakes up. The company members are sprawled asleep around him, and apart from the snoring, there's nothing to be heard.

In the morning the last of the logs are still glowing, crouched in the blackened throat of the fireplace. Outside, the wind has picked up and is shaking the bare trees on the hillside beyond. The season is turning.

Frankie and Beatrice set about charging the battery on the Mysterium's semitrailer under the open-sided barn. As of old, it will carry the huge roll of the big top, the banked seating. It takes an hour or so of tinkering and dry coughing from the starter motor, and then its engine suddenly grinds into life. Puffs of black smoke chug up from the exhaust as Beatrice revs it triumphantly.

Passing by, Darko glances at the belching carbon and grimaces. "Good old juggernaut, up and running again. Know where the word *juggernaut* comes from, Danny?"

"Doesn't it just mean a truck?"

"It's from Sanskrit. It was the name given to a massive wheeled chariot that got pulled by hundreds of devotees, and on it was a figure of Krishna. The World Lord. People threw themselves under the wheels and were crushed—"

"Less gassing, more packing," Rosa says, tapping Darko on the shoulder. "Have you seen how long this checklist is?"

Slowly a pile of rigging and rope ladders, counterweight harnesses, trapeze bars, and cables are piling up on the gravel.

"What about replacing Zamora's act with the full knife number?" she calls to Darko. "What does Sing Sing feel about it?"

"Way ahead of you," Darko says. "We're going to have a first practice in the barn."

"Danny, can you find the other walkie-talkie set in the cupboard in the dining room and take them to Frankie to charge."

"I want to watch Sing Sing and Darko."

"All hands to the pump on packing day."

He races to find the intercom equipment and spends a frustrating ten minutes untangling and sorting out the mess they've been left in. Dad would have a grumble about that! His task done, he dashes for the barn, keen to see how his sister's nerve will hold up. And slightly anxious too, he realizes.

But then that's the whole idea of an impaling act. It's meant to put your heart in your mouth. He knows how good Darko is, and he never really worried about Mum getting seriously hurt, even though he found it hard to watch. But this seems different now. In the old days he used to think the Mysterium's company was invincible, invulnerable to real harm, to death. Even though from time to time they heard of serious accidents, fliers paralyzed or worse, in other companies. But that was then . . .

He crosses the courtyard and enters the cool shadows of the barn. The swallows Mum loved so much are long gone, but the practice trapeze rig still hangs in place, tension cranked back into it in case the Aerialisques want to rehearse. Above that, at the top of the long ladder, the old hayloft is a thick shadow under the tiled roof.

Darko and Sing Sing glance up from where they're deep in conversation by the open knife case. She's changed into a white bodysuit, her toned arms and legs showing their strength and agility as she does a couple of stretches. The knife thrower has already set up his target board—the big wooden wheel with its rough red and black concentric rings. Danny goes over and runs his finger across the countless notches where the knives have struck. So many of them are gouged there that they pick out a hazy human figure where the "target girl" stands. No blades have struck there—apart from a cluster of deep notches right in the middle. Always the target will step away before Darko flings the last knife straight at the bull's-eye. For years that target girl was Mum. Now, her shape survives as a kind of negative—evidence of her bravery and steady nerve. (*She never even blinks*, Dad used to say, shaking his head. *How does she do it, Danny?*)

Sing Sing taps him on the shoulder, making him jump. Where her leotard ends, her skin prickles with goose bumps, he notes. The cold? Or fear?

"Seems weird, doesn't it?" she whispers, forcing a grin. "I'm going to follow in my mother's footsteps. Even though I can't remember her."

"Don't do it unless you really want to . . . You don't have to prove anything . . ."

"Just trying to help out," Sing Sing says briskly, looking round. Darko is standing by the knife case, warming up his throwing arm and going through that internal shift of focus and attention that Danny's seen performers doing all his life. Best left undisturbed now.

"It'll be fine," Sing Sing says and steps onto the foot rungs that jut from the board, spreading her arms wide, hands gripping the pegs to either side.

"See?" she beams defiantly. "Made to measure. I'm all grown up!"

Darko looks up, eyes sharp and alert. "OK. Remember, after the eighth knife you spin off to your left. I'll give a shout to make sure. And I'll keep them wide for your first go."

"Get on with it!"

"Give us a little room, Danny," Darko calls, "just in case there's a ricochet."

Darko's music stutters out of a boom box, and he suddenly springs into action, snapping into his routine. A cartwheel takes him to the case, his hand whips a blade from its resting place and then *thwunk*, it's flashed through the air and buried itself deep in the target board, a hand's width from Sing Sing's left knee, where it quivers. *I'm holding my breath*, Danny thinks. *No need. It'll be fine.*

Darko spins, picks two more knives and then flings those in quick succession, striking the board perfectly, just wide of the hip and then just below Sing Sing's outstretched arm. Does that right hand flinch ever so slightly, or is it just the force of the impact? Her eyes are scrunched half shut, and she's letting the breath seep between her lips, steadying herself.

Darko hesitates half a beat, checking that she's

OK, and then launches into a flurry of elegant throws that swish the blades across the gap to the target, and strike—*thump, thump*—left and right of his target's head, before working down the right side. The eighth throw is over his shoulder and hits a foot wide of Sing Sing's shin. It wobbles and drops to the floor as Darko shouts "Eight!" in a clear voice, and Sing Sing pirouettes off the supports and jumps to the floor. Half a second later, the last knife cuts through the air to strike the target dead center.

The knife thrower is bowed in a dramatic crouch. He looks up now.

"Ugh. Bad throw, that number eight. But you were great, Sing Sing. Really good for a first go."

Sing Sing pushes a smile onto her face, and hands on hips, she looks at the target board, appraising Darko's handiwork.

"You can go a lot closer than that, Darko," she says defiantly.

"We won't spin it yet," the knife thrower says, plucking blades one by one from the board. "Few days' practice to get you really confident. And I'm going to repaint the board this afternoon. I want to do this whole Tibetan Buddhist thing, a Wheel of Life image with reincarnation and karma. I was thinking about that last night when Zamora and I were talking. About heaven. Everything we do matters. We have to take responsibility for our actions—"

"I don't care what's on the board," Sing Sing snorts, "as long as you don't flipping hit me!" She looks more at ease now—as if she's passed some kind of important test.

Danny breathes out long and hard, turning away, not wanting Sing Sing to see how anxious he's been. *She's a tough girl*, he thinks. *Made her own way all her life, and she's not going to like being fussed over.* He goes over to the long ladder that leads up into the hayloft and looks up, thinking of all the time he used to spend hiding out up there, snug and safe, watching the company go about its business. He's about to climb up and take another long look at the code sheet, when Rosa's voice bellows out another order.

"Danny Woo! There's one handset missing! Where are you?"

"Coming!" he shouts—and trots back out into the daylight.

"I'll help you," Sing Sing calls. "Let me grab a tracksuit."

Darko goes to pluck his knives one by one from the board.

Thoughtfully, he wipes them clean on his trouser leg before placing them in their snug velvet grooves—and then glances up into the shadows above.

Responsibility for our actions, he thinks. *Amen.*

Somewhere up there, buried in the old rotting hay—the meadow flowers and long grass of last summer turning to dust—Jimmy's body lies cold and stiffening. The two silenced bullet holes that Darko put in his head last night already dried and congealed. His deep hooded eyes closed forever.

Mice, trying to fatten themselves for hibernation, are nibbling away at the cheese sandwich jammed in his jacket pocket.

By the time they've finished it and scuttled away to nest, Darko's freshly redecorated target board is securely lashed to a wall of the big semitrailer and the Mysterium convoy is pulling away into a long, cold night.

ACT TWO

WE ARE ALWAYS, EVERYWHERE, IN THE
HANDS OF THE PUREST OF MYSTERIES.

—*Franck André Jamme*

11

WHEN ANGELS SPREAD THEIR WINGS

Midmorning, under gray skies somewhere near Heidelberg, Zamora's phone pings loudly in Danny's pocket. When he slides it out, he sees a message from Inspector Ricard: *Will be in Berlin day after tomorrow. A man called Max may contact you. He is an old friend of Laura's. Has info. Take care. R.*

Danny's fingers quickly tap back a reply. *We saw Jimmy T. He was at winter quarters in France. And we are being followed—plate number 0354 CAM. Can you help?*

Nothing comes back for the next five minutes— and then the phone pings again. *Bike stolen a week ago in Madrid. The 49 perhaps? Be very, very careful in Berlin.*

Next to him, Sing Sing is cocooned in a pair of large yellow headphones, wrapped up in her own thoughts, and Rosa is engrossed in an intense conversation in Italian on her phone, hand gestures emphasizing every other word. Even Herzog—curled at Danny's feet, having chosen him as his traveling companion—is far away, locked tight in his own dreams, paws jerking and twitching.

Outside, the landscape and sky look ominous. Clusters of wind turbines, their long arms silhouetted, chop away at the thickening clouds overhead. In the dim light BMWs and Audis zip past in the fast lane, and on the highway shoulder, scraggy crows pick away at roadkill. Beyond them skeletal towers poke up from the fields and woods beside the highway. For hunting, Danny remembers Dad saying. A motorbike is overtaking now, headlight on full beam, and mechanically Danny's eyes fall on its number plate, just as he's checked every bike that's passed them that morning.

No match.

Near Leipzig, the first snowflakes flick against the windscreen. Just a couple of flurries, and they melt within seconds of hitting the glass of the warm cab or disappear as they strike the road. But it feels

115

like there might be worse ahead. Rosa puts on the main beams and leans over to fiddle with the GPS taped to the shuddering dashboard.

"Let's see how long to go," she says. "I'm beat. Arguing with my mum . . ."

She taps the *Time to Destination* icon, and Danny sees the digits ticking away. It's just flicked under four hours remaining. He does a quick calculation: 234 minutes and counting until he's back in Berlin. Will the Forty-Nine be waiting for them?

Rosa glances at him. "Don't worry, Bello. It's all going to be OK, I'm sure."

"Inspector Ricard says we need to be very careful."

"Tell you what—I could do your Tarot reading again. Always good to have guidance . . ."

The cards flash in Danny's mind, those startling images still vivid: the Hanging Man, Death in his armor. "No thanks. Not just now."

"Don't blame you. Not after last time. But maybe the cards . . . maybe fate has something better in store for you now?"

"I don't want to know."

Rosa smiles, dragging a hand across her tired, smudged eyes. "Well, I'll give you a prediction,

Danny. Despite everything, we're going to win the Golden Torch in Zirkus Berlin. We're patched up and battered, but we're still the Mysterium. The Mysterium reborn from out of the flames . . ."

She winces at her choice of words. "We'll win," she adds hastily, "and you can take the Golden Torch and go and show it to your mama and papa. Take it to their graves in their honor."

Danny groans. "But they won't know, will they?" Sing Sing has slipped the headphones down round her neck and is listening.

"Who can say?" Rosa says, crisply. "I was brought up the traditional way: good go up, bad go down. Blissful heaven, horrible hell."

"Mum always said dead is dead. Nothing more."

Rosa snorts. "Can't know, can we? Your dad would have said the big mysteries always lie just out of reach. And I agree with him. Keep an open mind. It's the best policy . . . I still talk to my papa, just before I perform. Sometimes it feels like he can hear me . . ."

Danny turns to Sing Sing. Something has been nagging away at his thoughts ever since they set out from Naudy, something he's been wanting to ask, but not sure how to judge the right words, the right moment.

"Will you come with me? To Mum and Dad's grave?"

Sing Sing bites her lip.

"I want to go as soon as we get to Berlin," he presses. "It really matters to me. And I'd like you to come."

Sing Sing puffs out her cheeks.

"Please, Sing Sing. I think you should—"

His half sister holds up her hand. "OK. OK, I'll come. For your sake. But I can't promise to be all warm and lovey-dovey about it. I want to forgive her, I do. But I can't. Not right now!" She bumps the armrest with a lightly closed fist.

"Maybe when we know why it happened," Danny says, "you'll feel better."

"Maybe. Who knows?" Sing Sing shakes her head. "But I'll tell you one thing: I haven't got a flipping clue what happens when we die. And I'm not in a hurry to find out."

Danny leans back in his seat and watches the clock on the GPS ticking remorselessly toward zero. He thinks again of Zamora talking about his island on that summer's day, about heaven, and remembers how he used to look up at that point under the hemisphere of the Mysterium tent—where the blue fabric stretched away tightly, curling out of sight, funneling to the top of the main posts. On a sunny day it glowed there, even though the rest of the tent was dark and moody, and he used to imagine it was the way up to paradise. You could climb the rungs on the support pillar and keep climbing up and up and up, through the clouds to a perfect place . . .

Danny is jarred to wakefulness as the trailer bumps over a ramp. The first thing he sees is the snow flickering in the headlights—and then a sight that sets his pulse bounding.

They're chugging through the Berlin Tiergarten, an expanse of tree-filled parkland in the heart of Berlin. Ahead of them, shining gold on top of her high column, Victoria—the angel of victory—spreads her wings against the sky. She glows in the last of the light, floating high above the woods and the traffic circulating around the monument's base. Beyond, he can just make out the Brandenburg Gate with its chariot and horses peeping over the bare treetops.

It all looks so beautiful in this fading light, in the falling snow—but then he remembers the danger that could be lying in wait for them amongst those trees. And in a great rush comes the crushing memory of the fire, the sense of helplessness and loss sweeping over him. *THIS is where it happened*, he thinks. *Right here in the park.* It feels so fresh again, the landmarks around them—even the weather—strengthening the emotions.

He turns to Sing Sing, wiping sleep from his eyes—maybe the hint of something more. "Dad used to call this the City of Escapes," he says quietly. "After the Wall went up during the Cold War, people tried everything to get out of East Berlin and into this part of the city. Digging tunnels, jumping out of windows. Microlight aircraft, balloons. Hiding in converted gas tanks of cars."

"And did they make it?"

"Some did. But lots were caught and thrown into prison. Or shot as they tried to get away."

"I could have walked across on a wire," Sing Sing says resolutely. "Zamora could have flown cannonball style! There's always a way."

"Not always," Danny says, his voice flat.

He jams the feelings back down and sweeps the ground ahead, scanning for anything that looks like trouble, a threatening reception committee.

They swing left, beneath Victoria's outspread wings, onto a road that runs toward the River Spree and then abruptly off that, into the park, directed by a yellow-jacketed marshal through a pocket of wood. The snow strengthens, flakes thickening the air as the semitrailer rumbles to a stop.

The air brakes let out a hiss, the engine stutters and dies, and the countdown on the GPS clock reads *0:00:00.*

12

WHEN NO WORDS CAN EVER BE ENOUGH

Danny spends the first hour or so pretending to help with the unloading, the unwinding of stabilizer legs on the caravans and trailers. But really he's keeping alert, watching the trees around them, the dark spaces beyond. Ricard's warning has only served to underline what's already clear: if they're going to keep safe, it's time to switch on every sense.

But there's nothing untoward to be seen: no hostile or watchful eyes, no gun barrels creeping round tree trunks—and no sign of Jimmy or that biker either. A little way beyond you can see Circus Cumulus setting up their dark red tent. The only visitors to the Mysterium encampment are a gaggle of smiling festival organizers and a couple of girls from Circa who've drifted over to say hi to Maria and the twins.

The snow is hesitating now, as if the clouds can't make up their minds whether to dump their weight here or save it up for somewhere farther away. A dusting has settled on the branches of the trees, the paths, but melted quickly on the grass.

Herzog steadfastly follows Danny wherever he goes. So much so that Danny starts to feel guilty and, passing Darko—who's busy rolling the target board down the ramp from the semitruck—he tries to urge the dog to go with his master.

"Oh, don't worry, Danny," Darko says, casting a quick look at Herzog. "He obviously feels you need the company. Maybe he knows what you're up against." He ruffles his dog's head. "Why don't we both take him for a walk later this evening? Just you and me. It's a lovely stroll past the monument, in the woods toward the Neuer Lake. Remember, there's that café there with all the log stoves?"

"Maybe," Danny says, glancing at the target board.

"Had to improvise," the knife thrower says, following his gaze. "For time's sake. Cut 'n' paste and covered in adhesive." He's done a fine job, though.

Scanned and printed images, from the Naudy library and the Internet, of Buddhas, mountains, streams, animals, are all plastered in concentric circles. And on those, Darko has hand-painted swirling stylized clouds and a sinister demon's face that hangs over the top of the board, his clawed hands gripping it at the sides.

"I'll improve it later," Darko says. "Let me know if you fancy that stroll, eh?"

Danny shakes his head. Ticking away under his watchfulness is the sense of urgency to get to the graveside—to keep his appointment with Mum and Dad . . . "I want to go to the cemetery as soon as we're pitched."

Darko nods. He watches Danny walk away across the site, then turns back to examine his target board. "Of course you do."

The festival roustabouts arrive in a minibus plastered with advertising for Zirkus Berlin Festival. The names of the companies taking part scroll around it: *Cirkus Bezirkus, CirkVOST, Cumulus, The Mysterium, Les Colporteurs, Cirque des Anges . . .*

Hired hands spill from the van, a dozen young men and women, putting on work gloves, wielding sledgehammers, eyeing the Mysterium's rolled big top, the scaffold for the main masts, the griphoists that will pull the tent into the air.

One of them looks older than the rest. There's a strong vertical groove stamped in his forehead, an exclamation mark of a frown that disappears under the black, woolly hat pulled down on his head. A bulky scarf is wrapped around his mouth and chin. He looks around sharply and then goes to join the others as they take their instructions from Frankie. He's come a lot farther than the others, and he can still feel the hundreds of miles on the motorbike tightening his stooping body. He stretches as he listens to the chief rigger, but his eyes keep roving hungrily across the pitch site, the gun heavy in his coat pocket.

Where's that boy gone now?

***

Just a few minutes later, Danny is leading Zamora and Sing Sing at a clip across the Tiergarten toward the triumphant arch of the Brandenburg Gate. He races three or four paces ahead and then waits impatiently for the others to catch up. *Just need to get this over and done with*, he thinks. *But what am I going to feel when I get there? Overwhelming grief? Or another kick of anger? If only the others would hurry . . .*

In a way it feels safer to be moving away from the encampment: the rising form of the big top is a giant sign to anyone who wants to do him harm. *Here I am,* it shouts. *Come and get me!* Still, even as it slips from sight, he measures up each figure coming toward him, trying to read their body language, their intent.

A lone cyclist veers suddenly in front of Danny, making him catch his breath—but then pedals away without another glance. An old man sits huddled on a bench, hiding something from view in his hands. But as Danny passes the man looks up, smiles, and reveals the packet of birdseed in his gloved hand.

Zamora is following at a steady pace, looking miserably at his arm, a few stray snowflakes settling on a replacement bowler hat. "Feel guilty not being able to help," he grumbles. "But you can't rush bone, right?"

The snow is dying out and the clouds lift a bit. Beyond the illuminated glass dome of the Reichstag, Germany's parliament building, you can even see the odd star and moonlight flaring the edge of a cloud.

"Is that it?" Sing Sing grumps, hands thrust in her pockets. "I've never seen proper snow before. Hope we get more."

"It can really come down here," Zamora assures her. "Bit early for that, though."

She pauses to look at the pavement, where an inset line of metal cuts diagonally across their path. "What's this?"

"That's where the Wall was," Zamora says. "Still up when I came here first. Man, it was weird—you could go right up to it on this side and wave at the guards in the watchtowers. Do graffiti. I sprayed a self-portrait! Only a few little stretches of it left now. Crazy how things have changed!"

But Danny's forging ahead toward the underground. "Come on!" he shouts.

"Jeez," Sing Sing mutters. "What's the rush? They're not going anywhere!"

"Now then, Miss Sing Sing," Zamora says. "This is hard for Mister Danny—"

"It's pretty flipping hard for me."

The Major sighs. "I'm not sure which one of you kids to feel more sorry for . . ."

It takes three trains to make their way across the city—through U-Bahn railway tunnels, through the cavernous, dizzying space of the Hauptbahnhof, through thick crowds that need to be scanned for signs of trouble. Any one of these strangers could belong to the Forty-Nine: the tattooed hipster who bumps into Sing Sing as he rushes for his train, the steely-eyed businesswoman staring at them from the opposite platform, the drunk staggering across their path. Zamora (ridiculously!) always attracts that extra stare, that extra glance—but now each of those looks must be decoded for any hint of threat. Danny falls silent as he concentrates.

Can't afford to let my guard down, he thinks. But as they slide back out into the night and the rendezvous with the cemetery approaches, he can feel himself withdrawing, going deeper inside himself. The faces on the train blur, the threat from the Forty-Nine dimming briefly, forced out by the immediate anxiety about standing at his own parents' graveside. They seem like strangers now, those people who lie beneath the ground. Not the straightforward Mum and Dad who were laid to rest in those pneumatically drilled holes, but people who were more complicated than he knew, who carried deep secrets within them. Mysterious figures . . .

At a flower stall, Zamora buys a bunch of red roses and glances anxiously into Danny's face. "OK, Danny?" he asks.

"Yep." Danny manages to smile back, but he's

not sure that he is. The ground feels soft under his feet, his head light and empty. Sing Sing has fallen silent as well and follows half a step behind, dragging her feet, chewing her own thoughts in her own private language.

A final clanking S-Bahn train brings them down the incline of Prenzlauer Allee and they get off, back into the cold night air. High above, the glowing bauble of the Fernsehturm glows atop its slender concrete tower, colors shifting through pink to purple to turquoise.

Zamora checks a map. "This way."

They pass through a gateway, through pools of light from the sparsely placed streetlamps—and into the graveyard. The moment—so long imagined, desired, dreaded—is finally on him.

But there's clearly been some kind of trick of the memory!

Danny remembers a grim space, starkly regimented, forbidding—but, instead, the cemetery's far wilder, softer, more quirky than he recalled. The graves are dotted between evergreen shrubs and small twisted trees. There are bird feeders hanging everywhere—from the branches, from posts, even from the gravestones themselves. Children's toys are placed on some of the plots—as if their owners had been playing with them and just stepped away for a moment. A white bike interwoven with dried flowers leans against a bench with a memorial plaque on it. Overhead, wind chimes ring in the swaying branches.

Even the gravestones are idiosyncratic: some are old railroad ties—standing vertically, names and dates carved or burned into the wood—some just big blocks of rough granite. Night lights and candles flicker in colored jars perched on top of some of them, and there's even a string of flashing fairy lights blinking pink in the shadows. Beyond the cemetery you can hear children in a floodlit playground on the other side of a wall. The whole thing feels—OK. Human. Cozy, almost.

"Nice, huh?" Zamora says. "An artist friend of Laura's suggested it. Thought it would . . . be a fitting place. Come on, lad. It's just over here."

He leads Danny gently by the shoulder and suddenly it's really there: he's looking at the grave of Mum and Dad.

The stone itself is a beautiful piece of polished stone, an elegant upturned U, planted solidly in the ground. It's riven in two, top to bottom, by a split in the rock—just a sliver, a long lightning bolt of a cut, perfectly done. Near the top, that split opens into a circle in which a glass orb is set, glowing softly.

"That's your dad's old contact ball," Zamora says, following his gaze. "Looks good, no?"

Danny nods, but his body's gone rigid. The emotion is taking hold, tightening, his throat thickening. Surely the feelings are going to break. He has a brief mental image of himself collapsed on the snowy ground, convulsed with sobbing tears, howling . . . He rubs a hand across his face and looks again. On the left half of the stone are the words HARRY WHITE and on the right LILY WOO, and below that, joining the two halves, a crisply cut infinity symbol looping backwards and forwards across the divide. Below that, in small neat letters, three words: EVERYTHING IS CHANGING.

Danny crouches down and lets his finger reach out to touch the stone, tracing the swirl of the infinity sign.

Deep inside, the sensation feels like it will overwhelm him, but then, as he traces that figure eight—once, twice, three times—his mind suddenly feels calmer. A kind of clarity returning, the threatened storm passing.

Where are they then, these people who were once his mum and dad? Rotting in the ground? Floating around in the graveyard like disembodied spirits? He thinks of what Rosa said about keeping an open mind, but try as he might, it doesn't feel like they're here. Where then? Everywhere? Nowhere . . . ?

He looks around at the night lights and bird feeders. Even the emotion in his belly is settling.

Weird that a bowl of soup should trigger so much emotion the other day, but this moment, which should be overwhelming, is OK, manageable.

But Sing Sing is clearly struggling. "It's really nice," she says, her voice tight, knotted in her throat. "Here, give me those flipping flowers."

She grabs them from Zamora, rips the cellophane packaging loose—and then sprinkles them hurriedly on the ground in front of the stone.

"Here I am," she mutters and pushes her palms together for a moment and bows her head—and then the tears start to flow. She turns abruptly and wanders away.

Danny watches her go, his finger still touching the cold stone. He closes his eyes and a snowflake brushes his cheek. Then another. When he looks up again, Zamora is gazing at him, his own cheeks speckled with tears.

"Ah, Danny. Sometimes there's nothing to be said, is there?"

Danny shakes his head. He feels he should do something more, say something, but it feels like that action—touching the stone—has done everything he needs to do. At least for now.

"Anything you want to say?" Zamora asks.

"No," Danny says.

"We can come back again," Zamora says, blowing his nose loudly. "No rush with these things. Where's that girl going?"

Danny looks around, but Sing Sing's already disappeared from sight.

"Come on, Major," he says. "Let's catch up to her." Much more important to talk to Sing Sing than the dead. More important now to look after his sister.

Back in the Tiergarten the Mysterium's midnight-blue canopy is pushing up to the top of its pylons. The night has brought the first proper snowfall—a steady down drift of small, restless flakes that scurry along the folds of the tent cloth as it tightens. It hasn't been raised since the last fateful Berlin appearance, but now—despite the association in Danny's mind—its familiar form lifts his spirits a bit. Over the year and a half he spent at school in England, he worried that the great mass of fabric would slowly be rotting in the storage barn at Naudy, but it looks all right. Only if you look closely can you see where it's been patched and mended.

The letters on the big sign punch into the gloom, and he thinks again how easy it will be for anybody to find them here. Friend or foe. He glances at Sing Sing. There's still the occasional shudder in her shoulders—the tail end of the tears triggered at the grave.

"Are you OK?"

"Yes," she says, not altogether convincingly. "I dunno. Thought I might ask her—Mum—about what happened. About that deadbeat gangster who was supposed to be my dad . . ."

"I can't imagine Mum would have had anything to do with someone like that," Danny says quickly.

"Like I say," Sing Sing sniffs, "don't know every-thing about her, do we?" But she seems to welcome the conversation now—and isn't shaking him off.

"Tell me something, Danny. Be honest. Did I look scared on the wheel? When those first few knives struck?"

"No."

"Liar."

"Well, just a tiny bit."

"I thought I was shaking so hard Darko would chuck me off!"

"You looked great. Honestly." Danny pauses and then decides the moment is right. *If we're walking into trouble, I want to do it with Sing Sing*, he thinks.

"Mum would have been proud of you, sister."

Sing Sing flinches—but then her face softens into a smile, as she nods her approval. "Thanks. How about you? How are *you* doing . . . Brother?"

That's good. Danny smiles. "I'm not sure. I'll need to come back again . . . but I'm OK." He pulls the scans of Dad's notebook pages from his pocket. "Right now I just want to get on with this." On the way back from the cemetery in Prenzlauer he's been turning things over, trawling his memory for anything that might give them an advantage. If the Forty-Nine are converging on Berlin, then the odds are going to be well and truly stacked against them. He taps the smudges beside the last, unsolved code.

Sing Sing squints at the paper. "What're you pointing at?"

"Dad rubbed some things out, but I can't read them. I was thinking we could scan the page again. And then boost the contrast and exposure on a graphics program. It might show up better."

"Worth a shot. Where?"

"Try the office in the Tipi Zelt," Zamora says. "Say it's for a prop or something and I'm sure they'll help. Here—you need one of these. Performer pass. And can you let me have my phone back? I need to make a call."

As he hands it back, Danny automatically checks the screen to see if there's another message from Ricard. A symbol shows an incoming call that hasn't been answered.

"Sorry, I think you had a missed call. I didn't feel it vibrate."

Zamora watches the two of them go, glad to see that they look more at ease with each other again, and then glances at the mobile.

"Well, I never!" the Major mutters and shakes his head, staring at the screen. He looks around. Wouldn't mind a bit of privacy to make this call. Danny and Sing Sing disappear round the side of the unfolding tent where a group of roustabouts are working a griphoist, tugging its long metal arm back and forwards, edging the tent to full height. One of them doesn't seem to be pulling his weight, Zamora notices. Typical! He's leaning on his sledge-hammer, watching the others at the hoist, but his eyes keep slipping away across the encampment like a gawker . . .

"Hey, you!" Zamora barks, marching across the whitening ground. "How about putting some effort into it?"

The man raises a hand in apology and starts to drive a long spike deep into the cold ground, the hammer sending metallic blows shivering back off the trees.

"That's more like it, *amigo!*"

But, as soon as Zamora's gone, the man drops the sledgehammer mid blow and then jogs off in the direction that Danny and Sing Sing have just taken.

13

WHEN EVEN STRONGMEN NEED PRIVACY

Danny waves his pass at the security on the Tipi doors and marches in. It's something halfway between a building and a permanent tent, with a lobby, a bar area, and a large cabaret space beyond. Izzy and Beatrice are perched on high stools at the bar with a couple of the girls from Circa, laughing uproariously, reveling in the warmth from a gas heater.

"Oh, Danny!" Izzy calls, her eyes sparkling. "There was someone looking for you—a Berliner called Max something."

Danny looks up sharply. "Where is he?"

"He had to go. But he said he'll be back later. Rather nice!"

Izzy gives her sister a shove. "Don't bother Danny with your drooling—"

"Did he say what he wanted?"

"No, but he said to give you this." She holds up a small brown envelope and hands it to Danny.

It has nothing on the front but the words DANNY WOO. He can feel something lumpy inside, padded by sheets of folded paper. He turns the envelope over in his hands—then nearly drops it.

Neatly done on the back are those familiar Forty-Nine dots in their seven-by-seven grid. But instead of a single one being circled, this time a noose has been drawn hastily around the whole pattern. And under it an emphatic question mark.

"What is it?" Sing Sing hisses as they stride across the deserted auditorium toward the office.

He shows the symbol on the back, and his sister pulls a long face. "Quick—open it!"

Danny holds it up to the light, trying to see what the contents may be, but the envelope is too opaque. He jabs his finger under the flap and tears it open. Something tumbles from the envelope, shining as it hits the floor: a key, stubby, a bit smaller than a typical household key, with a plastic tag hanging from it. Danny picks it up and reads

ALEXANDERPLATZ 16 neatly stenciled on the label.

"Alexanderplatz? What's that?" Sing Sing says.

"Sounds familiar, but I can't remember."

There's something still wedged inside the envelope: a sheet of folded newspaper, a raggedly torn page of the international edition of the *Guardian*. Danny opens it with quick, shaky fingers to see that an article has been circled in red pen.

GERMAN GOLD RESERVES
ON THEIR WAY HOME

The decision of the German government to repatriate its gold bullion—held in reserves in the US Federal Bank ever since World War II—raised eyebrows around the world. It seemed to indicate Germany's belief that America, long considered the safest haven for gold, may not be as secure as the vaults of the country's own Central Bank in Frankfurt. Under high security and secrecy, plans are already under way to ship billions of euros worth of bullion back "in the immediate future" . . .

Underneath—in the same red pen—someone has scrawled the words: *TELL RICARD IF I CAN'T.*

KEY UNLOCKS THE TREASURE! TRUST NO ONE UNLESS ABSOLUTELY SURE! SEE YOU SOON (Max A).

"Who *is* this Max then?" Sing Sing says, squinting at the signature.

"He's the one Ricard talked about in that last text."

"Any friend of Laura's is a friend of ours . . . ?"

"I guess so." Danny holds the key up in front of his eyes. "Let's get the scan done and then try and find what this key opens."

The office is up behind the Tipi auditorium. A young bearded assistant there checks Danny's pass and shows him over to a scanner connected to a laptop on a desk by the windows.

"Need some help?" he says. "I'm a big Mysterium fan. It's great you're—"

"Thanks,'" Danny says. "Just show us the graphics program."

The trees are huddled close to the back of the Tipi, and the snowflakes are drifting down, twisting in vortices of wind, forming ghostly shapes—then dissolving again. As the young man explains how to use the equipment, that movement outside flickers away in Danny's peripheral vision. It makes him feel uneasy somehow, but he concentrates again on the task in hand.

He waits until the assistant is sitting back by his own machine and then takes the scans from his pocket, smoothing them out quickly.

"The original would be better," he says. "But let's see."

He places the last sheet on the scanner bed and watches as the image forms on the laptop, Dad's familiar writing—the stubborn third code and clue—reproduced on the screen.

"Here. Let me," Sing Sing says, reaching across him. "I'm good at this stuff."

She drags the file into the graphics program, opens a control panel and quickly boosts the exposure and contrast. At once Dad's writing becomes darker, bolder—they can see the faint trails where his pencil lifted from the paper, thickening and becoming clearer.

Danny leans close to the laptop screen, squinting at the smudge near that last entry. "Zoom in on that, and boost it a bit more—"

He breaks off. In that moment, some kind of sixth sense stimulated, he's aware of that prickling sensation again. Like insects crawling on the back of your neck.

That sense that someone's watching you.

He glances round to see the admin guy apparently engrossed in the open spreadsheet on his own screen. No one else is in the room.

"It's coming . . ." Sing Sing says excitedly, fiddling the brightness up and down and zooming in on the blur.

Danny shakes his head and looks back over her shoulder. "Numbers," he says quietly. "Can you make them out?"

Sing Sing zooms closer, then squints. "It looks like *FQ 9354 kHerz*," she says, full volume. "A license plate?"

"Shhh," Danny whispers. Trust no one, Max's urgent note said. Maybe even this mild-looking admin guy behind them is watching. Listening.

"Herz couldn't be Herzog, could it?" Sing Sing says.

"Or car rental?"

"Excuse me," the young man says from across the room. "But that's a wavelength. A radio frequency."

Danny looks over, guarded, suspicious. "What do you mean?"

"You've got a radio frequency there. *Kurzwelle*— um, shortwave."

"What's that?" Sing Sing says.

"Type of radio wave. You get longwave, medium wave—shortwave are the ones that travel the farthest. Across the world if the conditions are right. My dad was an enthusiast, before the Wall came down. We were stuck in the East, but we used to listen to radio from everywhere."

Danny is still staring at the screen. *Doesn't make sense*, he thinks. *Why rub it out? Unless Dad wasn't sure—or was just jotting down some radio station he wanted to find again and didn't want to confuse me.*

And still there's that sense of being watched nagging away at him. Now, from out of the corner of his vision—out amongst the falling snow—he glimpses movement: lateral, urgent. He looks up quickly—just in time to see a tall figure dart away into the darkness under the trees, where he hovers for a moment, his face obliterated by shadow.

The motorbike man again. It must be! That same stoop, same angular movement. *He's followed us to Berlin then!*

His heart thumping, Danny turns back to Sing Sing, just as the door to the office opens and Darko comes striding in, his hair and shoulders dusted with snow, tugging Herzog sharply on his lead.

"Hey!" the knife thrower says. "Back already? Just need to print a few more things for my wheel." He registers the look of alarm on Danny's face. "Are you OK?"

Danny glances back to the window. The figure's disappeared—nothing to see now but the trees, the dark spaces between their trunks. *How long was he watching us?* he wonders. *What did he see?*

"I . . . I think I saw that man again. The one who raided our camp in Barcelona."

Darko throws his bundle of images down on a desk and dashes across the floor to stare out through the condensation-coated glass. "Where?"

"He went into those trees."

"You sure?"

"Pretty sure . . . I don't know, maybe not . . ." Danny says, his voice trailing off. Something's bothering him now. Even if that was the same man, that's three chances that he's had—three chances to attack. But, at each one, he's run away. *Maybe he doesn't mean us harm? Maybe I've been misreading his intentions and it's more complicated than that.* The way he carries his shoulders doesn't suggest aggression, or violence. More a desire for self-preservation. Fear even?

"Your eyes could be playing tricks in this light," Darko says. "But I'll take the Klowns—we'll go and have a sniff around."

Sing Sing joins them by the window. "Hey, Darko," she says quietly. "Any idea where Alexanderplatz is?"

"It's the big square under the Fernsehturm. TV tower," Darko says. "Why?"

"We found—"

Danny cuts her short. "Just got to meet an old friend of Laura's there." Instinct's kicking in again— no need to broadcast the story about the gold heist or the news of the locker key, with a stranger in the room.

Sing Sing looks at him sharply. "Oh, yeah. Sounded cool."

Darko looks from one to the other. "You two are up to something," he says shaking his head. "But you don't have to tell me. Just don't go haring off on your own. Take Zamora—or, better still, me. Especially if that guy *is* out there somewhere. I'll escort you two back to the camp, just in case."

Together they cross the frozen ground toward the Mysterium. The trees seem to Danny to have pushed that little bit closer to the camp, the darkness under them that little bit deeper. Under the great space of the tent there are now roustabouts and unfamiliar faces everywhere—but no one gives them a second glance, and there's no sign of that tall, thin man anywhere nor any motorbike parked nearby.

"Looks all clear," Darko says, turning to go. "But I'll round up that posse to check. Keep to the vehicles, OK?"

"I'll ask Rosa if she's seen anything," Sing Sing says. "Don't go anywhere without me."

"Don't worry," Danny says. "Like sister and brother we stand together . . ."

"What's that?"

"Chorus of our stupid school song at Ballstone."

"Sounds awful!" She grins and jogs away toward the caravan.

Danny watches her go through the swirling flakes, remembering Jamie Gunn standing next to him in assembly making up incredibly rude words to the tune. Seems like a lifetime ago now. Another life, entirely unreal—but then the older memories come crowding in again.

This must be almost the exact spot where it all happened!

You can see the Reichstag roof and the weird modern building near the river. *I stood almost exactly here and watched the trailer burning*, he thinks, and he turns slowly, through 360 degrees, matching what he can see now to his memory. The tent was there, the prop trailer there. Rosa's caravan maybe a little closer—and that was where the fire engines came and sucked water from the river—and that, surely, was where Danny saw Jimmy slinking away into the darkness. It was all real.

But now there's nothing to show. Not a trace of the scorched ground, the police incident tape, spinning blue lights, the sea of flowers that well-wishers came to place at the scene in the slushy snow. *Time is the greatest mystery of them all*, Dad had said, on that last visit to Berlin. He was distracted— bothered—but they had gone together to look at some bits of the Wall that were left, and he had looked, briefly, more like his old self, animated by his theme. *But it's what makes life possible, Danny. Even if we haven't a clue what it is. What one day is a matter of life and death can become a short, carefree stroll of a few minutes . . .*

Danny's gaze has come full circle back to the woods—and now he sees someone under the trees, a figure hovering just a few paces back but almost invisible. Cautiously, he moves closer to get a better look, out of the security of the Mysterium's arc lights and into the gloom, feeling like he's in no-man's-land, preparing to turn and run if he has to . . .

. . . And then he's relieved to see that it's Zamora, leaning against a tree trunk, his back to the encampment. Danny hurries across the freshly fallen snow to see the Major has his phone pressed to his ear, the shoulder of his good arm hunched as if to shield himself. Something protective—possibly furtive—in the posture, as if no one else should intrude. Danny can hear him talking rapidly in Spanish.

Danny pauses for a moment—and then strides under the trees. "Major?"

Zamora glances over his shoulder. "OK," he grunts quickly into the smartphone, "*Ciao, ciao,*" and thumbs the call end, before spinning round, his eyes glittering. "Can't a dwarf get some privacy around here?"

"Sorry—just need to tell you something important. You need to come back into the camp."

"OK." Zamora sighs. "Arm's hurting like the

devil again. Making me snappy. What did you want to tell me?"

"Who were you talking to?" Danny's blurted out the question before he's had time to check himself. The relentless, questioning part of his mind is running full speed again. Too many secrets held for too long. Now he needs to know everything.

"Just a friend," Zamora says tersely. "Now what's this news of yours?"

14

WHEN LOVE BLOOMS AMIDST CHAOS

An hour passes and the snow keeps falling.

A covering forms on the roofs of the Mysterium's vehicles, sits in white patches on the big top, making it look like an image of a cloudy world taken from space. Danny, Sing Sing, Zamora, and Rosa gather in conference round the table in the caravan.

"That's the guy I saw slacking," Zamora says. "He looked out of place."

"Just have to keep our guard up then," Rosa nods.

"Darko says there's no sign of him now. And we'll run a sentry system."

"And neither of you know or have heard of this Max?" Danny asks, showing the key with the

Alexanderplatz tag on it. "Or know what this key opens?"

Zamora shakes his head. "It's got to be a locker or something like that but no idea why you've got it. Wait for the morning. For one thing, it's got to be well below freezing out there, the snow's coming down—and that area around Alexanderplatz Station is pretty rough at night."

Despite the growing sense of urgency, Danny reluctantly agrees. He feels wide awake, eager to see what the locker key will reveal, but Sing Sing—tired from the journey or the emotion of the trip to the cemetery—is slumped against him on the bench seat. And he's not going without her.

"It's too cold to sleep in the prop trailer," Rosa says. "Danny, you and Major Z can bunk in here. We'll be snug. And safe."

Zamora smiles. "Just like the really early days when we used to cram six of us in here. I'm going to take painkillers and a sleeping pill and sleep like a dog."

Rosa sets about heating tomato soup on the stove, the blue gas flame purring, filling the tight space with a warming, reassuring aroma. Zamora does his one-armed best to pull sleeping bags from the lockers, until Sing Sing wakes and tells him to sit down and rest.

Danny studies the code sheet again, scratching his head as he tries unsuccessfully to conjure the numbers into any kind of sense. Giving up, he parts the curtains and glances out into the night just in time to see Joey prowl past—first sentry on watch duty—flicking a flashlight beam back and forth across the snow. *I don't care what that note said*, Danny thinks. *I trust this lot again. This is my family . . .*

And an hour later, soup warming his stomach, curled tight in his bag, he falls asleep—the Proust tumbling from his hand, its narrator in midsentence:

. . . I would go back to sleep, and sometimes afterwards woke briefly for a moment, long enough to open my eyes and stare at the kaleidoscope of the darkness . . .

In the dead of night, something tugs Danny insistently from sleep.

He sits bolt upright, out of the warmth of the sleeping bag and into the cold air in the caravan. The only light is coming from a small space heater that's struggling to lift the temperature.

Vrrrrrr–vrrrrrr. Vrrrrrr–vrrrrrr.

A shivering buzz in the silence. It's coming from Zamora. At first, Danny thinks the Major's snoring—or that his teeth are chattering with cold or pain or both—but then he realizes it's the phone vibrating.

Not wanting to wake his friend—not sure if he *could* wake him—Danny reaches stealthily into Zamora's jacket pocket and pulls out the shaking phone. *I'll just take a message if it's not for me,* he thinks, justifying his actions. But, in truth, he's burning to know who the dwarf was speaking to under the trees.

A single luminous green word reveals the caller's ID and pushes that thought instantly from his head: LAURA.

His fingers fumble to slide the answer icon and then he jams the phone to his ear. "Aunt Laura?"

"Danny! Is that you?"

"Yes. How *are* you? What's happening?"

"Why are you answering Zamora's phone? Where is he?"

"Asleep."

"Ha!" He hears Laura's familiar laugh crackle down the line, imagines her puffing the hair out of her eyes as she makes that explosive laugh. She sounds as Laura-ish as ever—just very distant. "Can you speak up, Daniel? Signal's awful."

"Don't want to wake the others."

"What others? Where are you?"

"Berlin. With the Mysterium. Sing Sing and Rosa—"

"What the devil is Sing Sing doing there?"

"It's . . . complicated. What about you? Are you still in prison?"

"Just been released. Ricard pulled every string he could between here and Hong Kong."

"He thinks the Forty-Nine might be heading here, to Berlin—"

"I know. Listen, has Max found you yet? Max Alekan?"

"No. But he left me a package. Is he OK? Can I trust him?"

"Pretty much. He's a . . . an old friend. Listen, just don't tell him more than you need to, OK?"

"Why not?"

"We're kind of rivals now. He's on the trail of the Forty-Nine too. Only tell him what you absolutely have to . . . He's a good sort, but he'll make a drama out of a crisis, believe me!"

The line fizzes—and then Laura's back on again.

". . . trying to get the first flight I can out of Rome tomorrow. I'll be with you soon. Cavalry's coming, Daniel. Just sit tight. Gotta go now. Police want me to sign something . . . *Si, si,* I'm coming. Keep your hair on, *Signor.* Bye, Danny. Be careful."

Danny stares at the silent phone in his hand, his heart lifted by Laura's familiar brisk voice, but frustrated not to have had longer to talk. If Ricard is on his way, if Laura's coming, suddenly it feels like the odds might just be slightly improving. Maybe it will all be OK. But what then? Back to some dull boarding school, the brief return to the Mysterium over and done?

He shakes the thought away. *No, I've made my decision and that's that! Laura can like it or lump it! And I need to take things one lock at a time,* he reminds himself.

His fingers are still hovering over the phone— and then he can't help it. He needs to know what was so secret that Zamora got all edgy like that.

Danny glances back at the Major, feels a shiver of guilt, then taps the call log button and scrolls down through the list. There's Laura's incoming call. Then before that, an unnamed phone number with a Berlin code. But the next outgoing call is listed as GALA.

8:52 p.m. That would match the time he saw

Zamora under the trees. The name is familiar—but it takes Danny a moment to place it. That's it: the other dwarf in Javier's beautiful photo of the company taken all those years ago. "We were an item once," Zamora had said before he choked up and changed the subject.

Quickly, feeling guiltier now, Danny tucks the phone back into his friend's pocket. *Just fed the bad dog again*, he thinks. He bites his lip and looks through the curtains. The snow has finally stopped, and the branches of the trees are lined with white. About three inches on the paths. A stillness hangs over everything, just like that moment on top of the Sagrada Familia. The world pausing in its spin . . .

And then, for a couple of seconds, he thinks he hears that child's voice reading the numbers again. Very, very faintly, as if coming from way across the Tiergarten.

Only for a moment—just a few words and then they're gone, cut dead mid-syllable on the frozen air. If they were even real. *Maybe Darko's right*, he thinks. *Maybe I am just conjuring things from my imagination.*

A second later, Aki goes past, wrapped tight in a woolly hat and big coat, a long metal tent stake shouldered sentry-style. Danny swivels on the bench seat to keep sight of the Klown as he swings round Darko's silent camper and is lost to view. A second later, he emerges on the other side and heads on toward the big top itself. He's moving forward faster now and almost out of sight, heading toward something—but his body is relaxed, not as if he's spotted trouble. The next moment Bea steps into view, and Aki drops the stake on the snow and the two of them wrap their arms around each other— and kiss briefly.

Don't like being a snoop, Danny thinks, closing the curtain. But it's reassuring for once to see a secret that isn't dangerous or threatening! Just life going on—two people falling in love.

He settles back into the warmth of the sleeping bag and lies awake for another hour—half an ear cocked for any hint of those numbers returning. But there's nothing more to be heard, just the lengthening silence of a snowy night, until—about one a.m.— there's a quick, familiar scratching at the door.

Chinking it open, he sees Herzog standing there, looking dejected and cold, wagging his tail.

15

WHEN THE FISH AREN'T FRESH

At first light Danny wakes Sing Sing, hurrying her to get dressed, eager to get going. He's been awake for an hour or so already, listening to the silence for anything alarming, turning things over in his mind. Now he can't hold back any longer the impulse to get to Alexanderplatz and find the lock that the little key fits.

Sing Sing grumbles herself into wakefulness, but the spark has returned to Danny's eyes, and one look into them convinces her there's no point arguing.

"We shouldn't go on our own," she whispers.

"I thought you were supposed to be the tough gangster girl. Besides, it'll be safer than hanging around here!"

As they squeak away across the new fallen snow, Darko swings round a corner, making his way back from the portable toilets.

"Ugh, freezing. Where are you two going so early, then?"

"Just to get breakfast. On Unter den Linden," Danny says casually. Any farther than that and he knows they'll be told to wait for an escort. And that might take ages.

"Listen to you. A true cosmopolitan traveler." Darko smiles. "Just keep your eyes peeled. Have you seen Herzog?"

"He's snoring next to Zamora. By the fire."

"Traitor," Darko says. "Sing Sing, we need to practice the knife routine one more time. And then you can be my target girl this evening. Your public debut with the Mysterium!"

Sing Sing beams. "You can spin the wheel, if you want to. I'll be fine."

They move on through the cold, gray light of a Berlin winter's morning. The first commuters are already walking the gritted pavements, a snowplow spinning orange lights as it nudges the previous night's fall off the grand street of Unter den Linden. Danny glances at the U-Bahn map, checks that no one is following them, and then they hurry down the stairs. No ticket barriers here, so no need for tricks—just have to hope no one checks, as they've virtually got no money left between them for the fare. Another biscuit for the bad dog!

He pulls a face as the U-Bahn doors close and they thump away into the tunnel. Sing Sing looks at him, her hands thrust deep in the pockets of a borrowed coat of Rosa's. "What's up?"

"Nothing. I thought I heard those numbers again last night."

"Why didn't you wake me? Then or when Laura called."

"I'm telling you now . . ."

The key with the locker number is gripped tight in his hand. "Wish that Max had stuck around," he adds. "Laura says he's a rival. Must be another journalist, I guess, but apparently he's OK."

"So why not stay to talk?"

"I don't know." Danny waggles the key in front of her eyes. "But maybe this will tell us. Got to be a locker key, right? At the station."

"Just hope it's nothing gruesome," Sing Sing moans. "I remember Charlie found a head in a gym locker once . . . it had been there awhile. Not nice."

"Why was it there?"

"Don't even ask!"

They ride on in silence. Danny looks at his sister out of the corner of his eye. Half the same flesh and blood, but such different life experiences. His, a life on the road amongst a (supposedly) tight and supportive community—hers, a harsh struggle for survival without parents amongst the rough gangster elements of Hong Kong. Heads in lockers!

As they ride up out of the belly of the U-Bahn and into Alexanderplatz Station, he sees fresh snow starting to fall and his heart ramps up a beat, the key still tight in his hand. "Did you see it?" he asks.

"What?"

"The head."

Sing Sing shakes hers in reply. But whether she's saying "no" or "don't ask," it's impossible to say.

In a café near the left luggage lockers, the tall, angular man turns his head to watch them rising into view on the escalator. Long, dark hair frames his high cheekbones, the groove on his forehead, the pale blue eyes staring at them intently. *Go for them now?* he wonders. *Or wait a bit and make it more theatrical?*

His fingers grip tighter round his Styrofoam cup, and the heat of the mocha intensifies on his palms. It's not the caffeine that's set his heart bumping, but the knowledge that—at long last—he's very close to his goal. The gun rests heavily in his trouser pocket as he glances round to see the snow ghosting down past the concrete thrust of the Fernsehturm.

No sign of the others yet. But they might have followed the children. They're professionals, after all. *Just need to be on my toes—and safer to do it here, away from the circus and prying eyes.*

Out across the square, past the base of the tower, a bruised white van is pulling up at the curb. Bold letters on its side declare its contents to be FRISCHE FISCHE—fresh fish—and a tall antenna jags into the cold air from behind the cab.

Crammed inside are six men wearing white overalls, rolled-up black balaclavas crammed on their heads.

The driver glances at his watch. 7:30 a.m. exactly.

He reaches to a shortwave receiver bolted to the dashboard and clicks it into life.

A short burst of chiming notes fills the cab—a nursery rhyme picked out on a glockenspiel: *twinkle, twinkle little star, how I wonder what you are.* The refrain repeats, and the man beside the driver reaches for a pad and a pencil as that slow child's voice starts to read off the German numbers.

"*Zwo . . . zwo . . . sieben . . .*"

Behind him, crouched in the back of the van, the other four men are pulling the balaclavas down over their faces.

Danny and Sing Sing are hurrying now, following the directions for left luggage, past the news agents and flower stalls, the coffee stands and cafés chugging out caffeine to buzz the city on its way. The signs lead them to the far end of the ground floor corridor and into a quieter space, a dead area with no through traffic, and they find themselves in front of a bank of lockers.

Danny's eyes scan the black numbers quickly. Number sixteen is a large one on the bottom row, big enough for the heftiest of suitcases. He takes a breath, then jiggles the key into the lock. It fits snugly, and as he turns it, they hear coins drop heavily inside.

For a second he hesitates, fingers resting on the handle.

"Go on, dummy!" Sing Sing urges.

"I was just thinking about that head," Danny says with a grim smile and then jerks the door open, bracing himself for anything.

16

WHEN COFFEE LOOKS LIKE BLOOD

As if the door of the locker is attached to him, the lanky man in the black suit leaps to his feet as it opens, straining to see what's happening. Now the boy's sitting back, scratching his head, and the girl's crawling deep into the locker's dark mouth, reaching for something. *Time to make my dramatic appearance*, he thinks. *Coast looks clear, so I'd better make my move.*

Three quick strides take him to the glass door of the café. His cold eyes flick back down the corridor toward the busier part of the station. Nothing to be seen but the ebb and flow of early morning commuters. *There you are*, he thinks, *there was no point worrying. As if Center himself was about to rear up!*

But then he feels a gust of cold air—behind him and to the left—and he spins to see the men in balaclavas pushing through the doors from the square.

Four of them. They're walking fast, arms held stiffly at their sides, presumably hiding weapons of some sort. This is not good. *But they haven't seen me yet*, he thinks. *I could just walk away. It's not really my business anyway . . .*

. . . But one glance back at the boy sitting on his heels—the girl wriggling backwards out of the locker—makes up his mind. They both look young, vulnerable. And it *is* his business after all these years!

Time to be a hero. Laura would laugh at that.

He strides quickly across the polished stone floor, jacket flapping, hand gripping the replica revolver. *Should have bought a real one*, he thinks. *But then what? Shoot someone? Not really my style! Theatrical prop'll have to do.*

Oblivious to the five figures hurrying toward them, Danny watches his sister drag the heavy object back out of the locker.

"What is it?"

"Suitcase. It's flippin' heavy, though—give me a hand, will you?"

She's crawling back out of the confined space, and Danny reaches past her to get a grip on one of the leather straps. As the light from Alexanderplatz spills onto the case, he recognizes it at once.

"It's one of Dad's!"

He sits back in amazement. "It's the one he always used on trips away from the Mysterium. What's it doing in there?"

And why wasn't it in the trailer? Why wasn't it burned to cinders like everything else?

"Must be his brick collection," Sing Sing grunts dryly, dragging it out into the light, its metal-studded feet screeching on the floor. "Quick, open it, dummy!"

But Danny's got his hand over his mouth, staring at the familiar stickers plastered to the dark brown case: ARGENTINA, RIO, I ❤ NY, CND, ROMA, HAMBURG, STOCKHOLM, BARCELONA, THIS MACHINE KILLS FASCISTS, ARCHAOS, ATHENS, ICH LIEBE BERLIN, DUBLIN . . . There amongst the jumble of images and words is one he hadn't noticed before: the red shield of Hong Kong and big letters *HK*. *He must have been there then—Dad must have been in Hong Kong,* Danny thinks. *Sing Sing doesn't seem to have noticed. Should I mention it now . . . ?*

"Come on!" she says, rattling the catches. "Get that lockpick set of yours working!'"

"OK. OK."

Danny flips out the S-rake and puts the tip of it into the case's lock. Shouldn't be hard to flip one of these. Assuming the mechanism hasn't rusted shut—the case is old, it belonged to Dad's dad after all, and the locker feels damp.

"Doesn't smell like a dead body anyway!" Sing Sing says, rolling her eyes.

Suddenly, hearing something behind them she looks round, and her intake of breath is so sharp that it stops Danny's hands dead.

"Big trouble, Danny!" she hisses, jumping straight to her feet. "Get ready."

Danny swings round, following her steady gaze. The man he saw last night in the trees—the one who's been stalking them for days—is racing toward them, a revolver in one hand, the other pointing frantically at four masked men who are closing in rapidly, pulling baseball bats, a long knife, a revolver from the folds of their overalls, their eyes fixed on Danny and Sing Sing.

"Run for it!" the man shouts.

One of the balaclavas reacts fast, veering toward him, baseball bat swinging. The black-suited man throws himself to the ground, and the blow misses, hammering into the bank of lockers with a resounding boom, denting one of the doors.

The others are almost on Danny and Sing Sing now.

"Come with us," the one with the revolver barks. "It's over."

Danny stares into his dark eyes, through the slit in the balaclava. "Are you with the Forty-Nine?"

Revolver just gazes back and raises his gun toward Danny's head. "Three . . . seconds . . . boy. Open the case."

Instinctively, Danny puts both hands on the suitcase, guarding it. He's not about to let the thing out of his grip. It belonged to Dad after all—and who knows what's inside! Behind him the thin man is back on his feet and is wrestling awkwardly with his attacker, trying to get hold of the flailing baseball bat.

"Why?" Danny says, trying to keep his voice calmer, deeper than it wants to be. Maybe he can bluff, buy a few seconds. "There's no point. There's nothing in it. It's empty," he lies.

The man hesitates for just a second and glances around at the others—and that gives Sing Sing all the time she needs to make a decision. She attacks.

A growl erupts from her belly, and she flies toward the man with the gun, catching him off guard, unleashing that same flurry of pirouetting kung fu kicks Danny saw on the peak above Hong Kong. She moves so fast the man has no time to brace himself, and the second kick connects solidly with his shoulder. Mr. Revolver gives a short, ragged scream of pain, and his arm jerks up and back, the gun detonating in the confined space, and the window of the café behind them shatters. The man falls, gripping his shoulder, arm twisted at a weird angle. From inside the café comes the sound of shouts, screams.

The other baseball-wielding man is already aiming a blow at Sing Sing. She drops into a crouch, hands on the floor, and the bat whisks the air over her head, missing by a fraction. In the same movement she sweeps fast with her legs and sends him tumbling to the ground, his bat spilling from his grip, rolling away across the floor to where it clunks the wall.

The man with the knife advances on Danny, blade jabbing away, backing him up against the lockers. "Got you," the man growls. He lunges forward—but, with a big effort, Danny lifts the case in front of him and blocks at the last instant. The knife thrust is fast and cuts into the leather, and for a microsecond, Danny is terrified it will come straight through and stab him. But then it shudders to an abrupt halt. There's the muffled sound of metal on metal—and the shock passes up the blade and into the man's arm. He looks surprised, and as Danny drops the case the knife is wrenched from his hand with it.

The man in black has managed to slam his attacker hard into the lockers, and it gives him a chance to scurry over to Danny.

"My name's Max. Max Alekan. I'm a friend of Laura's!"

So Max and the motorbike man are one and the same! *That explains why he didn't attack us.* Danny looks him in the eyes: "Why were you following us?"

"No time," Max snaps, looking at the attackers, who are regrouping, getting to their feet. He tosses his gun into Danny's hands. "Keep me covered."

Definitely no time for explanations. Two other jumpsuit-clad men have materialized from nowhere, one of them drawing his own gun from his belt and leveling it at them.

Sing Sing cartwheels across the floor and strikes hard at one of the assailants, snapping his head back with a straight-fingered blow. Simultaneously, Max rolls across the floor, grabs the dropped baseball bat, and launches into a frenzied attack. He's blocked by one of the balaclava wearers wielding his own bat, and they go at it like a couple of knights with wooden swords, the impacts sharp, echoing off the lockers. But the new gunman is training his sights on Sing Sing.

"Do something, Danny!" she screeches.

Danny stares, horrified, at the weapon in his hands. He's never fired one and it feels ugly, heavy. But he raises it, aiming at the man's legs—and pulls the trigger.

The thing bangs hard in his fingers and kicks back violently, so hard he nearly drops it.

But the man is still standing. No blood splatter, no wound, no effect from the gunshot as far as Danny can see. Except that now he is swiveling round toward Danny, taking aim.

Max is parrying blows from two attackers now, being driven back against the wall. "Get out of here, Danny!" he screams as he dodges a strike that chunks the wall above his head.

There's another gunshot: a metallic bang right by Danny's ear. He glances round to see a bullet hole punched straight into a locker. The sight of that gaping wound is all the urging he needs. He grabs the handle of Dad's battered suitcase with both hands, and with a huge effort staggers across the corridor, the weight of the thing dragging at his shoulders. Another shot rings out as he dives through the door into the café.

Customers are crouched on the floor, under the tables, hands over their ears. He can hear shouting behind him, Sing Sing yelling at the top of her voice. "Get off me, scumbags—"

She's cut off, and Danny hesitates. *Can't leave Sing Sing. But then again, it's either me or the case or both that the masked men are really after,* he thinks. *Maybe I can draw them off.*

The man with the gun is running to the shattered café window, taking aim at him again. Danny pushes urgently through the tables, tugging the dead weight of the case behind him, and dives behind the counter.

Another deafening gunshot. There's a clunk just above Danny's head as the bullet rips into the coffee machine, then an almighty hiss as steam bursts from the pressurized tank. It ruptures and coffee splatters across the wall like black blood. A young man is cowering behind the counter looking terrified. He sees the gun in Danny's hand and backs away, goggle-eyed.

"Exit?" Danny says desperately. "Emergency exit?"

The man points over Danny's shoulder. At the end of the service area, looking onto the snow-blinded square, is a fire escape. *I'll have to go for it,* Danny thinks. *Put a few warning shots over their heads, then try to make a run for it.*

He rises up on his haunches, keeping his head just below the level of the counter, aims deliberately at the ceiling and squeezes the trigger again, once, twice, three times. The gun barks each time, jarring in his hand. He expects to see chunks of ceiling tile fall at each shot—or exploding light fixtures—but nothing seems to happen. *Can't have missed the ceiling!* he thinks. *Must be blanks! Like Dad used in that old act of his.*

So let's go for it.

He stands, fires twice more at the crouching form of his attacker. Then he drops the gun, grabs the case with both hands, and goes barreling through the fire exit, setting an alarm squealing, out into the cold blast of the morning.

If I can just make it to the underground, he thinks, *into a more crowded area. Maybe find a policeman.*

But he's disorientated.

He half expected to see the beckoning steps of the U-Bahn in front of him, but now there's just the nearly deserted expanse of Alexanderplatz, the great column of the Fernsehturm in front of him. Everything is strangely muffled by the snow, his footsteps cushioned, the jagged voices behind him blunted. He glances back to see one, two, three . . . four of the balaclava men come rushing out of the station building. No sign of Sing Sing—or of Max.

Hope they're OK.

At least I've got a head start, he thinks, as his feet kick up the new fallen snow. But the case is slowing him down, banging away against his legs. Must weigh forty pounds—or more! He thinks about dropping it and sprinting free for cover. But some stubborn family gene is kicking in. *Something that links us all,* he thinks—*Dad, me, Mum . . . Sing Sing.* Determination. A pig-headedness that borders on stupidity at times, a refusal to give up.

The thought puts new energy into his legs. He rounds the base of the TV tower, sending a huddle of crows into disturbed flight just as a bullet chips the concrete support of the tower a few feet away. He sees the puff of dust before he hears the bang. *Need to go faster*, he thinks, *but I can't just outrun them, not carrying this.*

He looks at the curve of the tower base. As it reaches the ground it splinters into an array of walkways, escalators, galleried landings. *Maybe I can lose them amongst all that*, he thinks.

The snow's coming down more heavily again as he makes his way round one of the massive buttressed supports that sinks into the square. He glances back. For now he's out of sight—out of the line of fire—and he scans the building ahead, looking for a hidey-hole, for help of any kind. Ahead—about a hundred feet away—he can see orange lights spinning through the falling flakes, moving slowly along the road that borders the square. An emergency vehicle of some kind? Maybe that's a better bet than going to ground and waiting to see whether the Forty-Nine or the police find him first. It means breaking cover, but the gamble might just pay off. Danny takes a deep breath, tightens his grip on the case—and then powers across Alexanderplatz.

"Help! *Hilfe!*" he shouts, but his voice dies instantly on the thickening air. Away to his right, over the sound of his laboring breath, he can hear the rumble of another engine now. Looking round, he sees a white van bumping across the cobbled square, spitting up snow, closing on him. A jaunty fish painted on the side, smiling comically.

He transfers the case back to his stronger right arm and runs full pelt for the orange lights ahead. It's a snowplow: a squat vehicle, chunky tires spinning, its long blade shearing a ridge of snow before it, blue grit tank behind. Not quite the authority and safety he was hoping for, but maybe the driver has a radio and can get help. He glances back to see the white van, its headlights punching through the snow, almost on him. *I'm committed now*, he thinks. *But I'll be OK if I can make the driver listen.*

"Help!"

But as Danny accelerates toward it—just a few paces short—the plow abruptly rises and the vehicle changes gear, sending a chug of smoke up through its exhaust, getting ready to move away. There's a split second to make the decision. Behind the grit tank there's a platform and a short ladder. With five more long strides, his arm feeling as if it will tear from its socket, Danny covers the ground, feet skidding as they bite for grip through the fresh snow—and then he launches himself. Not perfect by any means, but his right foot finds a rung on the steps leading to the platform and his left hand gets half a grip—and he's aboard.

The driver clearly hasn't seen because he's accelerating hard now, pushing down the incline toward the middle of the city, the grand gray buildings sweeping by, whipped by the spinning orange lights. Danny tightens his hold and shifts onto the platform itself as they thump over the rutted snow, maneuvering the case more securely between his shaking legs.

Should have held onto Zamora's phone, he thinks, looking back over his shoulder. The fish van has briefly lost ground, but now it's accelerating and already starting to close the gap. He calculates options: no point jumping from the speeding plow—and no way to alert the driver. He'll just have to wait and see what happens, be ready for anything, any opportunity to get away.

They're at the bottom of the square now, turning right and then abruptly left, toward the river onto a long straight avenue. No hope that the van will lose sight of them. It's too close, and—with a slight skid—it takes the second corner, flashing its headlights and sounding its horn. But the plow driver is either still oblivious to the pursuing vehicle or incensed by it, because he's accelerating harder, wheels mushing the snow, across an intersection and then bumping over a bridge spanning the river. Just audible over the plow's engine and the hooting of the van, there's another sound now: the deep roar of a motorbike. Briefly, as the van jostles closer, Danny catches sight of a black figure closing down the long drag of Karl-Liebknecht-Strasse.

The river flashes past, then the bulky form of the cathedral looming out of the snow. Danny leans out to see what's ahead, and the cold wind whips his face. There's another, smaller bridge approaching and the buildings are denser beyond that, cluttered with blue and pink utility pipes.

But now the snowplow is braking hard, and Danny has to brace himself as it lurches to a stop. The cab door opens and the driver leaps down, shouting, evidently ready to confront the chasing vehicle.

The van behind brakes hard—too hard—and it loses its grip and skids, straight for the back of the plow. Danny heaves the case with all his strength toward the pavement and jumps clear, just as the offside front of the van slams into the back of the snowplow, its headlights splintering.

Danny doesn't wait. He rolls in the snow, grabs the case and makes for a side street that runs alongside this little offshoot of the river, the case banging hard against his tiring legs again, back into deeper snow. The weight of the case, the resistance of the ground, make it feel like one of those dreams where you can't run properly . . .

Glancing back he sees three of the balaclava men charging behind him.

They'll have him before he can find somewhere to take cover. A long, blank wall on his right, and no other way across the canal or whatever it is on his left. He glances down into the channel: no ripple of water, just a covering of snow blowing around across the mottled ice that's formed there. *Strong enough to take my weight? No idea how cold it's been here—or for how long. Can't risk it.*

The heavy-duty blue-and-pink piping—presumably housing for electric cables or gas—runs along the side of the canal. One, about fifty feet ahead, rises abruptly and crosses the ice-bound canal in a single span, before dropping to a tangle of pipes on the far side.

Easy enough to climb and cross the waterway—as

good as a bridge when you've grown up climbing ropes and rigging—but can he drag the case with him? And in this weather?

———————————

Sing Sing comes groggily to consciousness.

Her head's throbbing. For a horrific moment she thinks the blow has left her blind. Her eyes are open, but all she can see is thick, thick darkness— even when she waves her hands in front of her face. She reaches up to her head to feel where it hurts. No blood—that's good. Where *is* she?

Her legs are bent awkwardly beneath her body, and as she tries to sit up, she bangs her head and her elbow at the same time. It's like being in one of those contortionist boxes back in the acrobatic troupe in Hong Kong. But much colder! In fact, she realizes now she's shaking hard.

OK, calm down, calm down, dummy.

And then she remembers: the flurry of gunshots, exploding glass, the desperate struggle with three of the thugs, and then she felt the sickening dull blow resonate through her skull and she was slumping to the ground.

Now she kicks out with her feet, hears her shoes strike the metal door. *They've shoved me in the flipping locker!* She can just make out the chinks of light where the door doesn't fit snugly.

"Hey! HEY!" She kicks out hard at it, then listens hard. Not a sound.

"HEY!" she shouts again—and then the door swings open, flooding the inside with light, blinding her.

There's the aroma of coffee. A cacophony of voices. And a hand is gripping her by the foot and dragging her out into the concourse.

17

WHEN YOU'RE OVER THE BAGGAGE LIMIT

Danny reaches the pipe that stretches out across the frozen canal. Behind him the men are closing fast. But beyond them—beyond the white van struggling to disentangle itself from the back of the plow—he sees a familiar figure. Max.

Bent low over his motorbike, he's cruising across the bridge, boots out to steady himself. He's looking in Danny's direction. But instead of turning around and coming down the side street on this side of the waterway, he accelerates away, crossing the bridge and disappearing behind a parked truck. *Maybe he didn't see me*, Danny thinks.

He can hardly go another step with the case. Can't outrun the balaclava men while he's carrying it—probably can't even outrun them now if he drops it. The only way out is the pipe—but there's no way to shimmy up carrying that weight. Agonizing not to know what's inside: obviously something that mattered to Dad—or to someone involved with the whole story of his work for Interpol or the fire. The stickers stare back from the brown case, witnesses to years of travel, to secrets still unfathomed.

No time to open it—and the men will have him in a moment. The bag will just have to go— and maybe they'll go for that instead. Gripping the handle he swings it once, twice—and then hurls the thing as hard as he can down into the canal.

It lands with a smack and falls to its side. A hairline crack runs across the ice, but it holds, and the suitcase just sits there. *Maybe I could have run across the frozen water after all*, Danny thinks. And then he hears the bike engine carving down the street on the other side of the canal and sees Max waving frantically at him.

Relieved of the weight, given fresh hope by the arrival of the motorbike, Danny feels his energy returning and he throws himself at the thick pipe, shimmying quickly, rope style, to the top. It shakes a bit as he goes but seems sturdy enough. He's still bracing for gunfire—but nothing comes. Maybe they're out of ammo or don't want to attract more attention.

Wobbling, he steadies himself with one hand on the cross pipe, then rises up to standing position, kicking the covering of snow away to reveal a thin sheen of ice. *Not ideal!* But he spreads his arms and starts across as quickly as he dare. Although it's wide enough—almost like a balance beam—the slick plastic surface and fallen snow make it much harder. His feet jitter for grip, but he knows he just needs to keep momentum, keep centered, keep moving as fast as he dares, and he'll be across in seconds.

He glances back. What are his pursuers doing?

One of them is trying to clamber up behind him, but making a mess of it. Without the correct foot technique, it's impossible to get purchase on the smooth surface. Another is climbing down a ladder set in the canal wall, intent on retrieving Dad's suitcase. He edges out gingerly across the mottled ice to where the case rests in the middle of the canal. A loud, percussive crack comes back off the surface.

Danny looks down, but as he does so, his balance falters and his foot shoots off the slippery pipe. *Grab the wire, grab the wire!* Mum always shouted—even if you were on a low walk or had a safety wire. The survival instinct kicks in and he hugs the pipe as he falls, spinning around it so that he ends up hanging beneath it like a monkey, arms and legs wrapped tight.

Below him the ice creaks again. Then comes a longer, more ominous groan. A second later, the surface gives way in a rush—and the balaclava man, now just three feet or so from the suitcase—drops through the ice. Dark water blooms up, stifling his scream, and the crack grows rapidly, reaching out to the leather case—and then swallowing it. The man in the freezing water thrashes, but the heavy case goes straight down and is lost to sight.

Max is bringing the bike to a halt at the far end of the pipe, beckoning him across. Quick as his hands and feet can shuffle, Danny crosses the remaining stretch and then slides down the vertical part, like a fireman's pole, to the pavement below.

"Get on!" Max shouts.

Across the canal the remaining men are piling back toward the fish van, abandoning their colleague still flailing in the broken ice and water.

Danny jumps onto the passenger seat. "Where are we going?"

"Anywhere quiet and safe—I need a word with you." Max says, his eyes scanning the surroundings and settling on a sign fastened to a wall nearby. "Just remember the number of that building, for God's sake."

"Why?"

Max guns the bike. "Because you've just chucked about a million euros worth of gold in the Kupfergraben canal, Danny. That's why!"

18

WHEN THE TREEHOUSE BURNED DOWN

Sing Sing howls as she is dragged forcefully from the locker into the bright snowy light. It's hard to see anything, and she raises her arms to ward off fresh blows, sweeping her feet frantically to take a kick at anything she can find.

But instead, she hears Joey's voice, whispering in her ear. "It's OK, Sing Sing. It's just us Klowns. Bjorn and me."

"Where's—Where's Danny?"

"Darko just had a message from a friend of Laura's. He's got Danny safe—and they're heading to the airport to pick up Laura, apparently."

"Zamora lost his phone," Bjorn grunts. "He and Rosa sent us up here to rescue you."

"I could have done it myself!" Sing Sing huffs.

"Don't mention it!" Joey rolls his eyes.

Outside the sky is brightening, a lull in the weather, snow clouds thinning where the sun glows weakly beyond. The Fernsehturm shines in the morning light, and the concrete and stone of Alexanderplatz looks refreshed in its covering of snow. Sing Sing gets stiffly to her feet and plants her hands on her hips.

"So Danny's OK?"

"Apparently."

"What about the suitcase?"

"What case?"

"Danny's dad's suitcase."

"No idea what you're talking about. Come on, we've got to get you back to the Mysterium. There's a show to rehearse. And you're under house arrest, Rosa says."

Nearby, beyond the yellow-and-black incident tape, the shot-up café is thick with crime scene police. One of them peels away and walks toward them.

"Looks like you'll have to give a statement first, though," Joey whispers. "Don't say you hit anyone. Keep it simple. Just say you hid in the locker until it was all over."

"Someone bleeding well locked me in it!" Sing Sing grumps and then turns to face the policewoman.

Deep in the main buildings of Humboldt University, Danny and Max are sitting opposite each other in a student café. They've parked the motorbike in a service area behind the canteen and are tucked in a dark corner now, under a riot of posters and flyers for concerts, clubs, demonstrations.

"They won't find us here," Max says, stirring the sugar into his coffee. "We just need time to compare notes."

Danny plants his hands on the table, looks Max in the eyes. "What do you mean?"

"I need a look at those codes Laura sent you."

"Why?"

"Because with them I think we can win the war against the Forty-Nine." Max fires a quick, brittle smile at him. Almost apologetic. "And I think we can unmask Center."

Max's hesitation—the suggestion that he's trying to boost his own confidence a little bit—makes Danny feel bolder. "I've got questions for *you*. Why were you following us? Why did you steal Darko's stuff?" He pauses—and then taps the table firmly, drawing the man's attention taut. "*How* do you know Sing Sing's safe?"

"She was out cold. I bundled her into the locker and shut the door. Those creeps were always going to follow you. And the case. We'll go and pick her up."

"And what was that about gold? In Dad's case?"

"Two standard bars, Danny. Four hundred troy ounces each. At 950 euros an ounce, give or take, you do the math."

"But I don't understand. What gold?"

"Believe me, that's the least of our worries," Max says. He reaches inside the pocket of his black jacket. "Just answer me a couple of things, and then we'll get Sing Sing. We haven't got much time."

Danny shakes his head. "Can you prove you're Max. That you *are* Laura's friend?"

Max frowns, the groove in his forehead deepening. "Friend? We were more than that once. We were students together, studying journalism. I thought we were going to get married! Don't know what else to say."

"'So you knew her well then," Danny says

thinking hard. "In that case—tell me who burned down the treehouse."

Max looks perplexed—and then a smile flickers across his face. "It was your dad who did it. He was eight and Laura was nine—but she got the blame! Right?"

"OK." Danny shuffles in his seat. Remembers with a pang how hard Dad used to laugh when he told the story. He can't think of a better test—and he's warming to the man sitting opposite him. Max takes a sip from his coffee, his eyebrows raised in amusement. "I could also tell you some of Laura's other secrets!"

"What do you want to ask?"

Max pulls a dark maroon passport from his pocket and opens it to the photo page—and there's Darko staring back at them.

"Do you know this man?"

"Of course. It's Darko. And that's his passport. You stole it!"

"Borrowed. Just helping my investigations. I've been on the trail of the Forty-Nine far longer than Laura, Danny. I've been—everywhere. Just got back from Tokyo."

"But why steal his passport?"

"Darko Blanco's not his real name, you know."

"Of course not," Danny says, impatiently. "Almost everyone's got a stage name in circus work."

"His real name's Goran Dragovic. As a young man he was an intelligence officer for the Yugoslav secret services. At the end of the Cold War, he also worked for the Stasi—the secret police—here in East Germany. Then he went off the radar . . ."

Danny takes the passport into his own hands, staring at the photo, his pulse quickening. There must be some mistake, surely. Maybe Laura's former boyfriend has got the wrong end of the wrong stick entirely.

Max leans forward. "I think he's working for someone else now. That's why I put the note in your sleeping bag in Barcelona."

"Note?! I never found a note."

The man slaps his forehead. "Well—doesn't matter now. You know about your dad and Interpol, right?"

Danny nods.

"Well, Darko—Goran—may have been shadowing your father, feeding information to another source."

Danny sits back in his seat, the implication of what Max is saying hitting home. "Do you mean—do you mean the Forty-Nine? He can't be!"

"Maybe. But more likely he's working for another government. The Russians maybe. The Chinese. I'm not sure. He's either taking orders from—or monitoring—a numbers station."

"Numbers station?"

"They're mysterious radio signals. Started appearing just after World War I. Anyone can tune in to them—they're not scrambled or anything, but they make no sense. They broadcast on the same frequency every day—at the same time. People give them nicknames; Lincolnshire Poacher, *Atençion*, Russian Girl. The voices on the channels read out strings of numbers—code—probably from secret services giving orders to agents in the field. With a powerful enough transmitter you can send them halfway round the world. Criminal gangs do it too. I think the Forty-Nine are broadcasting on a numbers station. Darko has a shortwave receiver in his camper van—"

"I heard them!" Danny says. "In Barcelona. And I thought I heard them the other day. Dad had written a frequency down amongst the codes." Quickly he snaps the sheets of folded paper from his back pocket. But then he hesitates . . .

"But Darko saved my life the other night, on the

crane. So he can't be part of the Forty-Nine, can he?"

Max tilts his head. "Maybe he's not a danger to you—but he's certainly more than he claims to be. Think about it. If your dad was close to uncovering the Forty-Nine, other agencies would have been interested. Darko joined the Mysterium later than the others, right? He could have been planted. Now the Forty-Nine are after you—and those other powers may be watching to see who crawls out of the woodwork. It's a messy game out there. Not black and white. If Darko saved your life, then he must be lying in wait for the Forty-Nine. For Center. What else do *you* know about him?"

"He's from a long line of circus people. Great knife thrower. Used to do an amazing mentalism act."

Max shakes his head. "No. His father was a general in the Yugoslav army. Bit of a shady reputation."

Danny considers for a moment, mind spinning—then hurriedly spreads the sheet of paper on the table, jabbing his finger at the blurred radio frequency.

"Dad had guessed about the radio stuff. Look! That smudge says 9354 kHerz. Could that be the wavelength of the numbers station?"

Max whistles. "Right on! The Forty-Nine must have killed him because he was so close."

"But why are they still after *me*?!"

"Because . . . Because, A, your dad did something that upset Center so badly he wants to see your whole family perish. And B, I think you're holding the key to *his* identity in your hands." He points at the sheet. "Do you know what those codes say?"

"All but the third one. I can't work it out."

"Let me see."

Danny hesitates, then shoves the paper across the mug-ringed tabletop.

Max holds it up to the light. "Don't know. But if you put a gun to my head and I had to make a guess, I would say that's a book code. They're unbreakable if you don't have the right book—the right edition of that book—to crack them. Those groups of digits could be page number, line number, word number. Does that mean anything—"

But Danny's jumping to his feet. "I'm such an idiot!" he says, his eyes staring in anguish, lights firing green and brown deep inside them. "An idiot! It's the Proust! Of course!"

"Proust?"

"Dad left it for me. The clue said 'this one takes the biscuit'—it's the cake thing that the man in the book eats when he remembers everything . . . !"

He's already making for the door, pushing past the hipsters and students in line for coffee. All thoughts of Darko's hidden past—of Sing Sing even—forgotten in the urge to get back to the camp and decipher Dad's last message.

"Danny, wait! It's not safe. I'm going to call Zamora—Laura sent me his number." Max squints at his phone and scowls. "Hold on, will you?"

"I've got to get that book."

"Then I'll take you there on the bike."

As they round the back of the student union, Max stabs his finger urgently at his phone and jams it to his ear. It's ringing . . .

Neither he nor Danny sees the Frische Fische van wedged in the shadows of the access alley as they leap onto the bike. Nor the man who's leaning out of the passenger window, balaclava down and gun drawn, taking careful aim on the crook of his elbow.

Max kick-starts the bike, his phone still clutched in his hand, and Danny hops onto the passenger seat behind.

"No answer. Perhaps we'll just get down there as fast as possible. But I need to keep a low profile. I think Darko's on to me—"

Then something very odd happens to Max's hand. One minute it's holding the phone, the next it's as if it has exploded. Blood and bone flying, the phone spinning through the air.

Max's howl merges with the detonation of the gun. It takes a moment for Danny to work out what's just happened, that his new friend has been shot. Max half falls, half rolls from the bike, clutching the damaged hand to his chest, eyes rolling in agony, then seeking out Danny's.

"Go," Max murmurs. "Get out of here."

Now Danny sees three of the balaclava men advancing fast, the closest with his gun drawn. He thinks about turning and running back into the cafeteria, but then sees the gap they've left between the van and the wall. Why not take them by surprise?

Quickly, he slides forward on the seat and kicks at the foot lever, trying to remember how he watched Zamora do this so many times. At the second go he manages to time the clutch and gear shift just well enough. His right hand jerks the throttle open, and the bike leaps forward, crazily—much faster than he's expecting, much faster than the thugs are expecting—hurtling toward the van. There's a *thunk* as he clips the man with the gun, knocking him off his feet. For a moment he thinks he's going to fall and automatically sticks his legs out, braced for impact—but then the balance settles, and with a last-minute change of direction, he squeezes between the van and the alley wall, suspension chattering across the cobbles.

A fourth man is standing guard out on the street, but he jumps clear as Danny accelerates hard toward him, out of the gloom of the alleyway and into weak sunshine. He cuts a trail through the snow and slush as he crosses the road, narrowly missing another snowplow, then slides the bike hard around a corner. The engine is whining in complaint. *Need to change gear*, he thinks. *Is it down again with the foot or kick up?*

He looks down at the foot lever but wobbles, and as he swings back onto the road by the canal, he clips the curb. Heart sinking, he realizes he's lost control and the bike is sliding out from under him. The fall is almost slow motion as he and the machine sink to the ground, and then he's rolling in the snow, taking a cold mouthful, feeling the street ripping at him, before slithering to a stop. He hears the bike slam into something, the engine revving higher, and looks up just in time to see it catapult into the air and disappear from sight. A second later, there's the sound of it too crashing down through the ice.

Danny hauls himself to his feet and runs. They'll only be seconds behind him. In the distance another bridge crosses the canal—and now a cream-and-maroon train is rumbling across it. *Going the right way,* he thinks. *If I can just get on one of those, I can get back down to the Tiergarten and to camp. Then I'll confront Darko with what Max said—and get him to tell me what he knows. Use a mind technique if necessary,* he thinks, bravado strengthening his resolve for a moment. But it falters instantly. In his heart of hearts, Danny realizes Darko will be resistant to any technique—he knows it all too well.

The S-Bahn is slowing to a stop. If he's quick enough, he can probably just make it. His feet slap through the snow, and he risks a glance back over his shoulder. No sign yet of pursuit, but he's taking no chances and runs the length of the street full pelt until, at last, he throws his tired body onto the silent train.

Seconds later, the doors close—and then, infuriatingly, nothing happens. Passengers sit engrossed in books or smartphones, and the engine beats time for a full minute.

"Come on," Danny mutters, peering out of the fogged windows.

Is that it? A single headlight taking the turn where he lost control of the bike, picking up speed as it moves toward him? Looks like the fish van.

"Come on," he says out loud.

And then the train shudders and they're moving at last.

Danny slumps back into a seat and sighs out a breath so long and deep that he wonders if he's been holding his breath completely for the last hour.

19

WHEN NOT TO TUNE IN

Ten minutes later, he's jogging back under the Brandenburg Gate, cutting across the snowbound grass in front of the Reichstag. Inside its glass dome he can see people spiraling up the sloping walkway, hoping for a good view of the city. But the brief lull in the weather is over, and the sky is closing in again, becoming darker, threatening to obscure everything.

What will I say to Darko when I see him? Excuse me, but are you actually a Russian agent? Maybe he'll shoot me dead on the spot, Danny thinks. But he can't believe it. Even if Darko *is* something else than he's always pretended to be, the bond between them is real enough—surely? You can't fake that. Or the firm grip that Darko used to save Danny's life up on the crane, the light in his eyes as he pulled Danny to safety. Or could you?

Danny passes tents belonging to Circus Cumulus, to No Fit State—and then, heart bumping harder, he sees the word Mysterium looming, illuminated bulbs piercing the gray air on the freestanding arch that welcomes the public to the big top. Warm and inviting . . .

. . . But the camp itself seems to be deserted. Not a soul in sight.

He hovers on the edge for a moment, his eyes traveling across the big top, Rosa's RV, Darko's red camper, the two trailers, the minibus. The generator hums away. A couple of stewards in high-visibility jackets stroll into view, but otherwise, there's not a trace of the company.

He approaches the men.

"Where is everyone?" The older man shrugs.

"*Weiss nicht.*"

"Mysterium? *Wo?*" Danny tries again.

The younger man points away across the Tiergarten. "*Siegessäule.* The monument. *Fotos. Pressefotos. Verstehst du?*"

Publicity photoshoot for the circuses participating in the festival. Danny nods. *Maybe that's best. It'll give me time to do what I need to do. Crack the code. Then find the others at the monument and we can rescue Sing Sing and hopefully even help Max.*

He races through the hushed space of the big top itself, then checks the wings, the cabs of the other vehicles. He's definitely got the place to himself, and he runs now to Rosa's caravan, for the Proust.

Taped on the inside of the window is a hand-written note.

Danny—Gather all's well and Laura with you. Don't worry, Sing Sing fine. Back soon.

Zamora

Laura is with you? What's that about? And how does Zamora know about Sing Sing? Something's definitely not right.

Unusually, the door to the caravan is locked. But even with his hands trembling from the efforts of the morning, the flimsy mechanism takes no more than five seconds to pick.

Inside all is quiet—so silent that he can hear the bounding of his pulse, the soft brushing of the snowflakes on the front window. *Doesn't make sense about Laura*, he thinks uneasily, grabbing his backpack from the shelf. *She's on her way to Berlin, but she can't be here yet. And she's certainly not with me!*

It feels like the first time you run through a dress rehearsal for a new show and the whole thing's a mess and people miss their cues and get in a muddle. Just have to keep going and focus on what *you* have to do and—miraculously—the show works out fine in the end . . .

And the first thing I have to do is break the last code.

He opens the backpack and rummages for the envelope containing Sing Sing's birth certificate and the—now precious—Proust book.

But it's gone!

With quick hands and sinking heart, he checks all along the high shelf, under the table, even ransacking the lockers under the seat in case Rosa has found them fallen out of the bag and tidied them away.

No trace.

He looks up, confused, annoyed at himself. He should have got that clue right away. What would Dad have said? *Imbecile! I'm surrounded by imbeciles.* And now it's too late and someone's whipped them—unless Sing Sing or Zamora took them for safekeeping, which doesn't seem likely.

The snowflakes are tap-tapping at the window, and a fresh push of wind sighs through the trees outside. Was that something else out there? Another sound?

Like a soft footfall in the snow? Gently he cracks open the caravan door, eyes scanning for trouble, for the Frische Fische men, for anyone who doesn't fit.

No one. His eyes fall on Darko's camper van, sparking an idea that—once it has whispered its thought—he can't resist. *At least I can try and help poor Max find out more about Darko. And if the foreign agent theory is right, maybe he's got some evidence we don't have.*

He scurries across the ground to the camper van. The curtains are tight-drawn and he presses his ear to the window, listening hard. From inside there's a faint whimpering to be heard, but nothing else. No time for caution—this might be his only chance. He tries the driver's door. It's unlocked . . .

Danny's been in the camper countless times, and—in the old days—has driven thousands of miles with Darko, but now, weirdly, it feels like he's entering for the first time. With Darko suddenly transformed into an unknown and possibly dangerous man called Goran, this environment suddenly becomes transformed too. Unknown—perhaps enemy—territory. He squeezes between the driver and passenger seats and into the back of the van, to where Herzog is sitting on a bench seat looking miserable and cold. He wags his tail when he sees Danny, and gets up and stretches, the chain linked to his collar pulling tight. Darko never normally ties him up. That's really unusual—as was the way he tugged at Herzog's collar last night.

"Are you all right, boy?"

Danny ruffles the dog's head, but he's already scanning the compact, tidy interior of the van. Darko's possessions are neatly stowed—precise and ordered like everything else about the man. The knife case is the sole object on the Formica table. On a shelf behind that squats a high-tech-looking radio, all dials and equalizers, which Danny's never seen before. Its display is glowing, faint green in the darkened interior of the camper, and a cable snakes from that to a small box marked *Signal Boost 3000*. Next to that is a device with a red light over the letters *REC*.

Danny glances out through the curtains. Still no sign of anyone. So *let's see what we can find*. Maybe a clue to Darko's real identity. Maybe something more . . .

He goes closer to the radio and sees—as he has expected—that the dial is reading 9354. Cautiously, he turns up the volume and hears that disembodied child's voice telling off the numbers in German. "... *drei* ... *drei* ... *nul* ... *eins* ..." Herzog whines again.

"Shhh. Good boy. It's OK."

Danny's eyes fall back on the knife case. Normally it would be stowed away in the locked prop trailer, for safety. So what's it doing in full view in an unlocked vehicle? Maybe Darko's not so far away ...

He listens one more time to the faint whispering of the returning snow. In the silences between the hypnotic rhythm of the numbers station, he can hear it bumping butterfly-like against the camper, insistent, getting heavier, the generator rumbling behind that.

He crouches down to examine the two catches of the knife case, trying to see which pick he'll need to use. But to his surprise they spring open at the first touch, a loud *CLACK-CLACK* as they release one after the other—so loud Herzog's head shoots up, his deep eyes alert, glittering.

Danny takes a breath and lifts the lid ...

———

Joey, Bjorn, and Sing Sing are coming up the steps of the Brandenburg U–Bahn station into a fresh blast of snow. Joey glances at his watch, pulls his coat tightly around his neck, and grimaces. "Think we'll have missed the photoshoot. If they managed to do it in this weather . . ."

"When's Danny getting back with Laura?" Sing Sing mutters, rubbing the sore spot on her head.

Bjorn shrugs, striding into the teeth of the wind and the snow. "No idea. Rosa just wanted us to make sure that we brought you back safe."

"But he's OK, right?"

"Message was he's fine, Miss Sing Sing," Bjorn says. "Already told you that five times."

Sing Sing looks up at the falling flakes, feels her spirits lift a little. Laura's here, and Ricard and Interpol can't be far behind. They'll send those worms crawling back under their stones.

She tips her head back and spreads her arms. "My first real snow! And then my first performance with the Mysterium! Maybe it's all going to get better from here . . ."

20

WHEN YOU KNOW SOMEONE'S MESSED WITH YOUR HEAD

Danny stares in astonishment at the inside of the knife case.

But it's not the blades lying in their snug red velvet grooves that has gripped his attention: it's his—Dad's—copy of the Proust.

It lies there on top of the shining blades, almost taunting him. *Guess what I'm doing here?*

Darko must have figured out that it's needed to crack the code. But he doesn't have the sequence itself, of course. The original's still safe and sound back home—and the only other copy lies in Danny's pocket.

The numbers are still counting away in the

background, and Herzog's started to whine again. Danny looks at the book for a full thirty seconds, mind numb, almost unable to move as the voice slowly, slowwwly, intones its stream of syllables.

"... *neun ... neun ... acht ... sieben ... sechs* ..."

He's almost afraid to touch the Proust—but picks it up gingerly and, spreading the code sheet on the table next to the case, with shaking fingertips, turns the pages and starts to unpick Dad's last message.

<u>7.1.5 9.5.12 7.1.5 35.3.8 24.30.3</u>
<u>24.8.4 86.31.3:</u>
<u>13.20.2 + 132.11.1 14.9.8 + 132.11.1</u>

The first number: *7.1.5.* That means page seven, line one, word five. He flicks to the start of the book, finger tracing the first line: *I.*

Page nine, line five ... his finger racing now: *THINK.*

Same word as the first repeated now—*I*—then the next three come out as *KNOW WHO IS* ...

It's working! Page eighty-six. He riffles forward, almost dropping the book in his haste. Was that a sound outside? A faint scratch at the door? Quick ...

Line thirty-one. He counts as carefully as he can, down and down the page, then in three words: *CENTRAL*. That must mean Center, he thinks, heart bumping so hard he can feel it on the roof of his mouth. He probably couldn't find the exact word in his hurry. Now comes the colon in Dad's code. So this must be it. The reveal at last . . .

Page thirteen, line twenty. The second word is *DARK*—and when he flicks to the distant page 132 and finds the additional *OH!* that he is expecting, his knees go weak. And then, sure enough, the last two words read—with sickening inevitability— *BLANK + OH*.

DARK-OH BLANK-OH.

A siren is going off in Danny's head now, a kind of dizzying vertigo taking hold. As if only now he is seeing—like that sickening moment on the darkened crane—the immense void opening below him. *Have to get out of here, have to get out and tell someone!*

But a weird paralysis is taking hold. It feels as if his feet are stuck to the ground. His eyes drift across the camper interior, to the radio, that mesmeric voice right in his head now: ". . . *vier* . . . *drei* . . . *zwei* . . . *eins* . . . *nul* . . ."

And then his eyes fall again on the knife case. A thought had nagged at him as he picked up the Proust—and now he knows what it is. All ten knives are sitting snug in their slots. None missing. One of them must be the one that killed La Loca. Darko found it and didn't say. And tucked between them is Zamora's phone.

Danny! You've got to move! The voice in his head— weirdly, it sounds like Dad—is shouting full blast.

But he can't. Something about the radio, that other voice, the immensity of what he is trying to process, numbing his responses.

And then another realization strikes him hard. Of course! It was Darko who made Danny suspect Jimmy. That weird thing he said—back in the Sagrada—when they were discussing the fire, the sabotage. About looking for things that belong together. *Things that go together like jam and tea.* Jam and tea. Jam 'n' tea. Jimmy T.

All the hairs on the back of his head are rippling now, like he's being charged up with static—an electrical storm about to break. Darko planted the memory—all that talk about things that lurk in the shadows—

"So there you are, Danny," a soft, familiar voice

whispers in his ear. "Time we took a little ride, you and I."

Danny, lost now in that incessant voice on the radio, the falling snow, the confusion in his mind, turns round and looks straight into the eyes of Darko Blanco. His pupils are two burning black diamonds.

"Shhhhhhh." Darko hisses and moves swiftly.

One hand reaches up and forces Danny's head down, planting his forehead against the palm of his right hand.

"Sleeeep!" Darko's voice is resonant, authoritative, taking full control. "Your head's heavy. Heavy. Eyes closing!"

Danny knows immediately that Darko's using a snap induction, but try as he might, there's nothing Danny can do to fight that heaviness. The radio voice must have had some kind of effect, pushed him toward the hypnosis. Interesting, there's no fear. Just this almighty heaviness, numbness. But it can't happen like this, can it? A flicker of resistance in one corner of his brain still. Dad always said that you couldn't be hypnotized if you didn't want to be. You couldn't be made to do things that you didn't want to do, and most of stage hypnosis has to do with social expectation, peer pressure—trying to be helpful.

But I want to run now. To scream. To fight. And I can't. Maybe Dad was wrong then . . .

Maybe Darko's just very strong willed . . . Maybe he's primed me for this . . .

Maybe . . .

Darko is guiding him to the seat just behind the driver's and is strapping him in.

"Buckle up, Danny. Just a quiet ride. You and me. In the snow that's falling down and down and down . . ." Darko's singing out the words now.

And then the camper's engine is churning to life and they're off, bumping across the encampment, a little skid of the wheels now, and then it's smoother and the engine *purrrrrrrs* as Darko changes gear and pulls away, accelerating into the soporific, smothering snowfall.

ACT THREE

IN HEAVEN, EVERYTHING IS FINE.

—Peter Ivers

21

WHEN THE NIGHTINGALES SANG

When Laura finally disembarks at Schönefeld Airport—disheveled, relieved to be out of custody, panicking that she is too late—she runs like she's never run before. Sprinting across the tarmac to the head of the line, she flashes her passport at border control before snatching it back.

Forget the stupid suitcase, she thinks, spinning past the baggage carousels, barging through the other passengers. Cold air slaps her face as she exits the terminal and virtually bodychecks a businessman out of the way to grab the next taxi in line.

The driver starts to protest, but—seeing the fierce look in her eyes—thinks better of it. *"Wohin?"*

"Tiergarten. Tipi Zelt. And be quick about it. *Schnell, bitte!*"

The cab pulls away as she drums her fingernails on the armrest.

First we roast, and then we freeze, she thinks. The snow's falling steadily on the birch woods, lining the branches with white. Even the crows look cold as they hop on the verge beside the road.

Just need to get to Danny, she thinks. *Why the devil isn't Zamora answering his phone?* She scrolls to Max's last text—a mistyped jumble of words: *In bag trouble Danny escarped im hurt Humboldt U. Help.*

Never could rely on that man, she thinks. *Dope. Hope he's OK, though. Haven't seen him in so long.* For the briefest moment she remembers summer evenings on Unter den Linden—twenty years ago now—walking hand in hand. There were nightingales singing in the trees, and the city had just been reunited.

Forget it! Ancient history.

Danny escaped. From something, someone. So where is he now? Only place to start is at the Mysterium. Everything revolves around that. It's a center of gravity pulling everything into it. Destroyed Harry and Lily. Laura won't let it take Danny too.

She leans forward, puffing the hair out of her eyes. "Can we go any faster? Pleeease?"

The camper growls on through the falling snow, heading east, across the old line of the Wall, Darko keeping up a running commentary, like some sort of hypnotic tour guide.

Bewilderment in Danny's head, his attention slipping from the view outside to what Darko's saying in that low monotone of his—and back to the city again.

". . . so you found our radio station," the knife thrower is saying. "It really is a wonderful method of communication. My operatives keep me informed of everything from our base. We're about to get hold of a ton of gold, Danny. A ton. The two bars your dad stole from us can lie at the bottom of that canal for eternity for all I care . . . On the left you will see another Cold War tourist trap . . ."

Berlin slides past: grand gray stonework, cranes raising a new building beside an empty lot full of weeds bending to the snow, a line of old Communist-era cars painted pink, mauve, yellow, zebra stripes huddled below a sign saying *Trabi Safari*. On previous visits this city had thrilled Danny. Now it seems vast, scary, utterly disinterested in his own fate. Some shop windows are already bright with Christmas figures and lights. Normal life flowing around this bubble of weirdness inside the camper.

Darko swings them round another corner, accelerating smoothly.

". . . Just listening to my voice. You can't speak now, Danny. I'll give you a chance if you're good and sleeeepy now . . . So where was I? Oh yes. Living out our destinies, like I said the other day. Victims and killers and knife throwers and secret agents. Cause and effect. Harry and I agreed on that at least! When he exposed *my* father, it led to Papa's death . . ."

Is that a slight catch in his voice? The words tangled for a second on the sharp edge of an emotion? Darko coughs. "And that led to Harry's death. And so on. And now—in a minute—you're going to tell me where that precious notebook of your dad's is hidden . . ."

They're turning east now, about to cross the river again, the city opening up into wider, snow-whitened spaces.

On the right, a jumble of color: a long stretch of the old Wall itself, but for half a mile or so, every inch of concrete has been painted with bright graffiti. A spider's web, a view of Mount Fuji, two old men locked in an embrace, swirling question marks spiraling into the very center of a snail shell. Behind it, you can just make out a balloon, mottled blue and white like the earth, stamped with the words *DIE WELT*.

Was that the one I nagged to go up in? Danny thinks hazily. *That last time?*

"Here's the East Side Gallery," Darko says, his voice lifting, taking up again the role of tour guide. "When I was in East Berlin, we didn't have graffiti on our side. Everything was clean, ordered, proper. I wouldn't want to go back to that, though, even though I was a top dog."

But Danny's mind is fighting now. Maybe that shift in Darko's tone—or the hint of emotion—has loosened the hypnotic grip of his voice.

"Wh—Why did you kill La—La Loca . . . ?"

"Covering my tracks."

"But—But it was you . . . who started . . . the fire?"

There's a silence from Darko. Just the hum of the engine, the steady counting, Herzog whining. Then the voice comes again. "At first when I saw you'd escaped I thought, well, good luck to you. But the more I thought about it, the more I wanted to scrub out Harry's existence. You're a part of him, of course. Part of his project, if you like. So, in the end, sorry to say, that meant you had to go too. Quiet now. Shhhhh!"

Danny makes one last effort. "Ricard . . . knows . . . it's you."

"No, Danny," Darko says firmly, "he doesn't. The only other person who was close to me was that bad seed Max. And we've got him nailed. Eyes shut now."

Danny slumps again and his eyelids are heavy, but he just manages to keep them open. The colors of the gallery blur and come to an end. The camper turns, over a tangle of railway lines, black ribbons in the snow, across the shivering river again. Big blocks of houses here. Expanses of plain wall have been covered with huge graffitied figures: babies, monsters, flowers, spacemen, all some four or five stories high. Nightmarish in the gloom.

"Not far now," Darko says. "We're going to an old Stasi prison. Not the one they've turned into a museum, but a smaller one everyone's forgotten about." He pulls a bunch of keys from his pocket and rattles them.

"But guess who has the keys! Keep listening to them ringing, Danny. Jingling. You're going deeper now. Deeper . . . eyes closing . . . roll up . . . roll up for the Mystery Tour . . ."

And Danny can't fight it anymore. His eyes are closing and his head nods forward. At the last moment before sleep, his whole body dragging down, giving up the fight, he half remembers something Dad said about hypnosis. *Some people say that if you repeat something over and over in your head, you can block out the suggestion, Old Son, but it's probably nonsense . . .*

Anything's worth a try now! So in his head he starts to sing the lines Darko has prompted. He remembers them blasting out from the speakers, introducing a show long ago, when he was no more than four or five, and the world seemed so immense and wonderful and safe.

Roll up! Roll up for the Mystery Tour. Roll up! Roll up for . . . roll up for . . .

And his eyes shut.

22

WHEN ZAMORA DANCED ON THE TABLE

In Danny's head he's gliding through the falling snow now. Past the orb of the Fernsehturm, the mighty grid of the streets below, out over the woods, the river and train tracks, the golden angel Victoria on her monument.

Ahead he sees the great Mysterium semitrailer.

Its doors are open, the ramp down—and he swoops into its black mouth, into a long, dark tunnel, sliding deeper for what seems like hundreds of feet, and then—at the far end—he can see a brightly lit disc. Small at first, it grows bigger and bigger and bigger as he sweeps toward it.

And suddenly he finds himself standing before a giant version of Darko's Wheel of Life. It's turning slowly, steadily, the figures on it picked out in red and gold and green and blue, the animals and people all revolving with scrolling, stylized clouds. Above it a demon's head, mouth widening into a grin, holding the spinning disc, leering at him . . .

A loud click in his ear. Another.

"Wake up now. Wake up."

Darko's voice is brisk, businesslike.

Danny opens his eyes. It's a surprise to find himself awake again, his body shivering hard with fear, cold, shock. Still that tune looping in his head. He tries to hum it, waiting for his vision to clear.

"Wake up, Danny."

They're standing in some kind of compound. A pungent smell filling his nose: the odor of freshly dug earth.

Gray walls tower above, topped with rusty skeins of razor wire. There's a path running around the edge of the small courtyard—and in front of him a scrubby, weed-filled flower bed, its roses long gone to ruin. A shovel sticks up from a heap of freshly turned soil.

Danny breathes hard, trying to bring the shivers under control. He's already worked out what that dug earth means, but he's doing his best to push the thought far away. He looks up into the downdrift of the snow, letting the flakes ghost against his face, their cold touch waking him a bit more. Overhead the sky is blank.

Darko snaps his fingers one more time. "I'll do you a favor, Danny. If you answer quickly and truthfully, perhaps I can reconsider."

Don't look at him. Don't answer.

"Danny? Are you with me? Pay attention!"

Danny lowers his gaze, breathing deeply, steadying himself. There are other figures clustered around the knife thrower. Three men in jumpsuits—could be the same men who attacked at Alexanderplatz. But his eyes are drawn to the small figure standing just behind Darko. It takes a moment to pull the man from his memory—and then he recognizes Kwan, his enemy from Hong Kong.

So somehow he survived the sharks in the South China Sea!

None of those unpleasant smiles from Kwan now, just a steely look in his eyes. "You messed up my big operation, boy," he says quietly. "My big payday!"

"That was nothing, Kwan!" Darko snaps. "Right, Danny. Tell me: where's that notebook? We know it survived the fire. That you had it. You told a boy at school about it—and we gave him enough money to make him tell us how you used to boast about it and the codes and secrets in it. And enough for him to tell us your schedule. A sensible lad—what was his name now? Jamie? Glad we missed him with the bomb."

Jamie Gunn! Jamie was in on this—or at least a tiny part of it. Danny swears under his breath. But it's more astonishment than anger. After all, that bomb at the school had nearly killed him too . . .

"Speak up!"

"I don't know where it is. Laura gave it to Ricard—"

"That's a lie, Danny," Darko's voice sings. "I was better than your dad at this. I can tell a lie at a hundred paces. Just by the way you set your head. And I can see how many times you blink from here. Tell me where it is."

"No."

"Then we'll find Laura—make her tell us."

The snowflakes are settling on Darko's salt-and-pepper hair. His own emotion is easy to read, Danny notes. His control is wavering—and there's anger, rage ripping up out of him.

"TELL ME! Or Sing Sing dies. In full view

of everyone, on the target board. 'Oh. Sorry, Mr. Policeman, it was a terrible accident,'" Darko quotes in a plaintive voice. "'My nerves were all shot to heck because I was so worried about the missing boy.' Perfect crime really—"

"OK." Danny snaps. "I'll tell you."

He knows there's no chance of the knife thrower letting him live—and the situation is clear. But if he can save his sister? It feels like that might at least be possible. Then at least a part of Mum survives—a part of our family . . .

Danny's eyes move, hesitantly, to the pile of earth in the old flower bed. Sure enough, there's a yawning hole next to it. He swallows hard. "The Escape Book is at Laura's house. In my room."

Darko kicks the ground angrily. "We checked there. Turned it over while you were in Hong Kong. Don't mess me around."

"There's a secret drawer under the desk. Laura knows where it is, but it's hard to spot."

The knife thrower slaps his head. "What did your dad always say, Danny? Pay attention to details, right? That's why the Forty-Nine planted me in the Mysterium. That's why I got promoted to Center. And that's why I spotted Harry was on to me."

Danny nods, but he's only half listening. Darko may have decided his fate—but *he's* made his own decision: he's not going down without a struggle. And Danny's thinking of Dad's advice now—keeping an eye on detail. Maybe—just maybe—that will give him a way out.

As his head clears he scans the courtyard, checking how many men are guarding him (three), how many guns he can see (two), how many doors there are out of the courtyard (one—a small squat door with a barred window). Herzog is standing by that door now, scratching at it, as if eager to be away. He looks back at Danny, tail planted between his legs.

"OK!" Darko says sharply. "Look at me now, Danny. Nothing to fear!"

Uncertainly, his knees turning watery, mouth dry, Danny looks back, Darko's voice compelling him to meet his gaze. Perhaps he's going to do a snap induction again—

And then there's a sickening crack on the back of his head, his skull shaken by the blow—and he falls to his knees, his body going limp, stars weaving amongst the snowflakes in his eyes.

Darko's voice somewhere above him. "I've got

to get back now. You know what to do. Come on, Herzog!"

There's silence—and Danny fights hard, trying to keep up, above the black undertow pulling him down . . . More distantly, Darko's voice again, spiked with impatience: "Herzog! Come! Herzog! Well, stay here then, if you care so much about him. Stay here and rot for all I care . . ."

And there's a yelp then from the dog, the slamming of a door . . .

Mustn't go under, mustn't go under, Danny thinks. *If I lose all consciousness, I'm done for. But if I can fight that numbness in my head, there might just be a chance . . .*

Herzog is barking incessantly now. "Shut up!" someone shouts at the dog.

Danny feels his body being lifted. Strong hands heaving him into the air, across the courtyard, toward the open wound in the ground. *My head hurts so much,* he thinks. *But I'm aware of it, so I'm still thinking. If I still know I'm thinking, I'm still conscious. Got to keep awake. If I open my eyes, they'll shoot.* Perhaps he'd better take his chances in the earth. Perhaps he can do what Dad never could . . . living burial.

He needs to keep his mind active. Distract himself from the fear that spooked even Houdini . . .

231

And now he feels the cold radiating off the earth—the grave—as his captors half drop, half lower him down. The smell of the soil engulfs him. *Doesn't feel that far down,* he thinks, his hopes rising a fraction. As the men release their hold on him and he sags to the wet snow at the bottom of the hole, he moves his arms and legs, just a fraction, experimenting to see if they're still under his control. Yes, just about. He wiggles his toes in his trainers, shifts an arm from under him. He can hear the men muttering overhead. Herzog is still barking but less sure of himself. Heavy snowflakes settling on his body.

Just have to wait, he thinks. *Can't try anything yet.* His head is throbbing and every instinct is screaming at him to get up and get out of the grave, but he knows he would just be shot where he stood. He has to wait until Kwan and the other men think the job's done and leave. Any thought will do to keep the mind busy, keep it from looking right into the face of the demon spinning the Wheel of Life—and Death—in front of his eyes. *Mustn't start dreaming or I'm lost . . .*

Snow falling, snow falling . . .

He reaches for the memories, grabbing at seemingly random images and thoughts:

Rain thundering on the empty street in Hong Kong. Hail pinging off the car roofs in Paris.

Mum gliding through the air, against the starry backdrop of the tent—against the stars themselves at Naudy. Quiet Sundays there, the white table set outside for dinner.

Zamora dancing on that table one night, celebrating his fortieth birthday with a dance so crazy that the whole thing collapsed. And everyone laughing.

That look on Sing Sing's face under the Barcelona moon, just days ago, astonished, fearful, vulnerable. The moment he found he wasn't alone . . .

Mum and Dad holding hands late one night after they had argued, silhouetted against the Mysterium's illuminated lettering, some of the bulbs blown and Dad saying, *Nothing's ever perfect, but it's pretty good a lot of the time . . .*

And—inevitably—his thoughts loop back to Dad, struggling from a shallow pit, his first or second go at the living burial, spitting, coughing, failing to control the panic after just a few spadesful.

No way, no way. I'm going to have to think about this, he said, his voice jagged with alarm. And he jumped up from the grave, brushing the soil from his shirt and trousers, breathing in the clean air of a spring evening. Darko was helping shovel the earth. "It can't be done, Harry," he had said, certainty ringing in his voice.

So I'll show you, Danny thinks. *I'll show you, Darko!*

Gritting his teeth, he breathes deeply, charging his muscles up with oxygenated blood, flexing, getting ready for what is to come.

There's a sound above the grave now and Danny braces himself. He risks parting his eyelids very slightly, squinting up through the snow melting on his face. Two blurry figures are looming over him. They make a sudden movement and then everything goes very dark. But it's not earth. Just a foul-smelling piece of old carpet or something. It lands heavily on him—a bit of a shock—but an idea comes almost immediately.

It's like any escape, he thinks. *The weight of the earth will stop me from moving, but if I can make some slack, it might just be possible. And this shield will help.*

Danny waits, surprisingly calm now that a plan's forming, listening hard. There's the sound of the shovel biting earth and then—*thwump*—the first spadeful hits the carpet. He feels its weight and braces himself more firmly, trying to preserve as much room as he can under the carpet.

Whump! Another spadeful. Then another—and then they're coming thick and fast. The impulse to move quickly becomes unbearable.

They think I'm out cold, Danny thinks. *So I've got an advantage. Need to make the most of that.* And the hole didn't look as deep as he'd feared. *Need a breathing hole.* Cautiously, he rolls onto his side, then eases his right elbow and knee up, lifting the foul-smelling covering to make more space for himself.

But as the soil falls, shovel after shovel, the weight starts to scare him. Already his muscles are trembling with the effort of keeping those life-giving spaces, his nostrils full of the smell of the earth.

Hold your nerve, Woo, he thinks. *A few more minutes.*

But that look on Dad's face keeps coming back. Not often you saw Dad scared to his socks, Zamora said. But he was terrified that day.

Push it away! Think about Sing Sing. You've got to fight your way out and make sure she's safe.

The soil is pressing down, harder and harder, his breathing pocket squashing shut, soil seeping round the sides of the covering, pressing in toward him. *Can't wait anymore. Got to get out!*

There's just enough space left to wriggle sideways and work his way to one side of the hole. Chances are the earth will be less compacted there—they'll be chucking most of it in the middle. His fingers claw the crumbly, cold earth, working it down past his front and then pushing, kicking it away with his knees and feet, like a mole. But it's hard to coordinate and the soil falls against his face, pushing the panic button harder.

Help! Help!

No, it's OK, I can still breathe. As long as I keep my head turned away.

He squirms harder, out from the carpet and suddenly his nails are clawing at what feels like solid rock. Must be the undisturbed compacted earth, the edge of the hole.

The weight's crushing his ribs, but there's still just enough slack to move his limbs. Time to dig up. Can't wait another second, and if he comes out too soon, then so be it. At least he'll have died trying. Better than just lying here.

The anger's returning now, fueled by everything he's had to endure these last two years: secrecy, lies, abuse, all the violence and anger directed at Darko. And it's helping him. That great ball of righteous anger welling in his stomach, firing his limbs. An energy that can be used.

Frantically, summoning everything left in his reserves, he claws his way upward, like he's swimming, fighting for the surface through water thick as mud. Every single inch is a struggle, a supreme effort of will and courage—but he's making progress, he's pretty sure of that.

Are they still filling it in? He hesitates, his heart straining in his ears, listening for the tell-tale bump of earth above, perhaps to feel its impact. Nothing.

But it's a mistake.

In that moment his arms lose power and the weight of the earth feels like it's leaning down with renewed intensity.

Can't breathe—soil in his nose, mouth . . .

He can see stars again now, jumping across his vision, and everything going white.

Consciousness fading . . .

Every single thing fading.

23

WHEN THE SIGNAL'S STRONG

Laura's taxi is caught in a traffic jam. Nothing's moved for five minutes and the snow is coming down with real intent. The car's windshield wipers are struggling with the weight of the compacted flakes on the window. They clunk back and forth, and the driver puts on gloves and a hat and gets out to chip them clear.

"Are we getting anywhere?" Laura shouts, peering through the windows into the woods beyond.

The driver gets back in and shakes his head. "Bad weather," he growls, then turns round. "I think two cars crash into each other."

"Can I walk from here?"

The man raises his eyebrows, looking at Laura's

light clothing. "Half an hour. Very cold out there."

"If you knew what I've been through," Laura says, buttoning her jacket tightly and pulling out her wallet. "Could I buy your gloves off you, my friend? Maybe that nice hat too. Name your price!"

Not far away, in an unmarked office in central Berlin, a group of technicians are clustered around their equipment.

None of the Interpol men have eyes for the snow piling against the plate glass windows—or the view of Under den Linden beyond. Instead, they're all focused on a heavyset man clutching earphones to his head with one hand, tuning a dial with the other, his gaze fixed on the laptop ticking out numbers before him.

"Well?" says one of the watchers, an older man with a hangdog face. "Is it them?"

The man with the headphones nods. "*Ja*, 9354 kilohertz again. We've got it triangulated off three masts now so we can ping it to within a few feet. They've been on the air almost nonstop—the signal's almost off the scale."

"How close?"

"Probably coming from within the city, Herr Direktor."

The older man straightens up from the screen. "Has Ricard landed yet?"

"They've just closed the runway at Schönefeld— but maybe he'll get in at Tegel."

"We can't wait. The tip-off says they're planning the heist for tonight, so we've got to roll as soon as we get the location. Give the order to shut down the cell phone network—in case they're using that to call back into the base station."

He gazes out into the snowstorm to where the Brandenburg Gate is drifting in and out of sight. As for the boy Ricard's been worrying about—probably doesn't stand a chance, poor kid.

And beyond the Brandenburg Gate, deep in the Tiergarten, the heat blowers are working hard to pump warmth into the space under the Mysterium's hemisphere. Sing Sing, Joey, and Bjorn are greeting the rest of the company returning from the snowed-out photoshoot.

Zamora bustles up to Sing Sing, pulling her close with his one good arm in a powerful hug. "You're OK. And Danny's found Laura apparently. You haven't seen my phone, have you, Miss Sing Sing?"

She shakes her head. "Where did you say Danny is?"

"With Laura at a hotel. She phoned Darko. I lost my phone."

Sing Sing's looking round, puzzled. "So where's Darko?"

"He had to go and see a client. Something urgent to do with his business. Rosa let him go because the photoshoot was such a nonstarter. *Brrrrr*, it's freezing in here."

Rosa, bundled up in multiple layers, comes through the curtain, her face grim. "Can't really rehearse the aerials in this temperature. More bad luck—who'd have thought this would blow in so early in the winter? Hope Danny's tucked up somewhere warm with Laura. We'll work through some things and do Darko's routine as soon as he's back. As long as you're ready, *Bella*?"

Sing Sing nods her head. "I'm ready for anything."

24

WHEN THE GOOD DOG BARKS

A wild but muffled barking brings Danny back into some kind of awareness, refocusing his clouded mind. Under the ground. Living burial.

Not a hint of light and that downward pressure still crushing his body, but he feels warm now, bizarrely. And, apart from the distant sound of Herzog, there's nothing to be heard. So quiet under the soil. Almost restful. Tempting just to give up the struggle and let everything go with it.

His hand is jammed in front of his mouth, but instinctively he's cupped it to make a breathing space.

Not dead yet then . . .

I've got one last effort in me, he thinks. *I'll give it everything until I black out again.* He starts to wriggle, twist, jerk his limbs—and, yes, there's a hint of movement, the soil slipping over him, around him, under his squirming body. Feels like he's inching upward. But how far to go? A foot? Three feet or more? If it's the latter, then he's toast, he knows that. *My last trick will end in failure—my last Mysterium act* . . . On gloomier nights, Dad used to say that every act eventually ended in failure. Either you got too old or your time ran out . . .

But now the anger comes welling back, full force. One final surge of fury at the events that have rained down on him and his family. How dare they? How dare they take Mum and Dad? How dare Darko or Goran or whatever his name is destroy the wonder of the Mysterium!

A weird animal growl fills his throat and transforms into a ragged cry, half scream, half shout as he claws again at the soil . . .

". . . rrraaaaarggggggghhhhhhhhh . . ."

And now he can feel the earth is suddenly looser and something's above him, moving, a sharp scratch snicking across his face, cutting his cheek, a violent motion in the soil. He braces himself for the onslaught of the blows or bullets, pushes himself upward with everything he's got left, ready to fight, tearing clear of the earth.

And then, in one glorious rush, he simultaneously feels the cold air slapping his face—and hot dog breath, as Herzog's tongue rasps across his nose and mouth.

The dog's barking frantically now, claws still digging at the last of the soil—and Danny's hands and arms and face are free of the grave, the last of the roar choking in his throat. Herzog licks at his face again, tail wagging furiously.

"Good . . . boy . . . Good . . . dog . . ." Danny gasps. He's sitting up, legs still half buried, blinking in what light there is, snorting grainy soil from his nose and mouth, while Herzog goes crazy. It's a joy just to breathe freely—to feel his lungs and ribs expanding fully. "You helped me! You good boy!"

Danny hugs the cold, wet dog tight. Shielding his eyes, he looks around. No one to be seen in the grim prison courtyard. Just the blank concrete walls shutting him in, razor wire, tumbling snow. The watchtowers empty against the fading afternoon light.

His head still hurts, he realizes, but who cares about that? He just wants to breathe this lovely cold air and feel Herzog's wet snout nuzzling at him. Life! Life in all its wet, cold, and aching beauty!

But then he remembers Sing Sing. *Can't waste another moment*, he thinks, looking round frantically.

No way to scale those walls. He pulls himself free of the clutch of the earth and staggers across the snow to the thick cell door, eyeing up the lock and tugging the pick set from around his neck.

Slightly out of breath, Darko materializes from out of the shadows of the big top, brushing snow from his hair, his shoulders. He glances at Sing Sing and the others, a phone clutched in one gloved hand, the knife case gripped in the other.

"Sorry to take so long," he calls. "Sing Sing, we need to rehearse the knife number. I'll just warm up by the heater for a moment. Frankie, can you and Rosa set up the wheel for me?"

"What's the rush?" Rosa moans. "We might have to cancel the show tonight at this rate."

"It'll be fine," Darko says. "Worst is already passing apparently. We've got to get this routine looking slick. We're professionals."

Lurking in the shadows the freshly painted board glows with its clouds and animals and Buddhas.

"Might as well," Sing Sing says. "But I'm keeping my tracksuit on for rehearsal. Too cold for a leotard."

"Let's get on with it then," the knife thrower says briskly. "Thought we could spin it today. Not too fast. If you're brave enough."

Sing Sing looks him in the eye. "As fast as you flipping well like, Mister Blanco. I'm a tough fortune cookie. Wish Danny were here to watch."

"You'll be together soon enough," Darko says and snaps open the knife case.

It takes five long minutes on the first of the locks for Danny to realize that it doesn't do anything. There's no real mechanism inside, just a satisfying *clunk clunk* as you turn the lock, as if its maker wanted the door to look and sound worse than it actually is. *Illusion*, he thinks, cross with himself for falling for it. Psychological stuff. He puts his eye to the frame of the door, checking each lock in turn—and there, from the bottom one, a black tongue of a bolt thrusts across the space. The only real lock in the door.

He cranks the tension tool and tries the S-pick, fiddling it deep into the hole, feeling for any movement. It's a guess—but a good one—and with a *snick* the bolt pulls back into its socket at the third attempt, and the door's open. Herzog bounds through it, as if eager to be clear of the courtyard. No sound in the long, dim corridor in front of them, and nobody to be seen. *Surely they'll have placed a sentry,* Danny thinks.

"Herzog! Here, stay close, boy."

A row of cell doors leads off to both sides and, set high in the wall, a line of red lightbulbs all connected to a looping wire that rises and falls like a telephone cable, reaching away into the gloom. Herzog's looking up at him expectantly, still panting from his furious digging, waiting for a signal.

Follow those, Danny thinks. *Must be an alarm system, so they must run toward a control room, a guardhouse.*

At first, he advances slowly, ears alert for the slightest sound that indicates Darko or Kwan is waiting on guard.

But the place feels utterly deserted, desolate. Cautiously, he tries a light switch. Nothing. Then tugs the alarm cord, bracing for the siren—but the wire simply comes away in his hand.

No idea where I am, he thinks. *And time's running out.* He starts to run, limbs still heavy, trying to push images of Sing Sing and those razor-sharp throwing knives from his mind. But he keeps seeing that last impact: Darko flinging the one that strikes the board dead center. At the heart.

By the time he's reached the far end of the interminable corridor, he's sprinting, feet banging so hard on the bare floor that he almost doesn't hear the shouting coming from the last cell on the right.

"Help! *Hilfe!*" The voice is strained, fighting for strength. Desperate to be heard—but still familiar.

Danny stops, swivels the spy hole in the armored door—and sees Max staring back at him. "Help! Let me out!" He's hammering on the door now. "Get me OUT!"

"Hold on!" Danny shouts, but the man just keeps up that racket on the other side, dissolving in full-blown panic.

This lock's much harder. Danny's fingers fumble, struggling with the mechanism, panicked by the sense of passing time, by the nonstop banging from Max on the other side of it.

Maybe I can't do it, he thinks. *Maybe I should just leave him and get going? But he might be bleeding to death. Can't just leave him a second time.*

He tries one last time with the rake and then the

lock gives and the door flies inward. Max pushes past, his mangled right hand wrapped tight in an old, bloodied towel. "Danny! I thought I was going to suffocate in there. Where are they now?"

"It's Darko," Danny barks. "Darko's the Center. He's going to kill Sing Sing."

"Then let's go," Max says, gritting his teeth. "There's no telling what he might do, Danny. He'll be desperate to carry off their gold robbery. How dare that piece of scum stink up my beautiful city!"

Danny's already moving toward the barred gate blocking the end of the corridor, and Max hurries to follow. "We'll stop him, Danny. For your Mum and Dad." *Yes*, Danny thinks. *For Mum and Dad. And Javier. And Charlie Chow. And that decent inspector who went to the bottom of Hong Kong Harbor. Who knows, maybe for poor old Jimmy. And most of all for Sing Sing, if—*

No, don't think it. Not yet.

There's a simple padlock round these internal gates, and Danny's pick rips it open in seconds, rattling the thing back on its tracks.

"This way," Max shouts, leading them down a short flight of steps, through an unlocked door and into a kind of loading bay.

"How do you know?"

Max grimaces. "I was in here once. Years ago . . ."

At the far end the vehicle doors are cracked open—as if Darko and the rest have left in a hurry—and, pushing through those, they find themselves in shin-deep snowdrifts, the wind gusting, tumbling the snowflakes around them. A single set of tire tracks leads away from the prison, already blurring in the renewed fall. Herzog bounds ahead barking, waiting every now and then for them to catch up, suddenly eager and excited again.

Nothing in sight except deserted, graffitied tower blocks staring down at them, windows blinded where the glass is missing.

"My hand's a mess," Max says, clutching it tight to his body. "We need some help. But these old Stasi blocks are empty."

The area around the prison is forbidding. They pass through an abandoned gatehouse, between silent warehouses. The wind has real teeth to it now and the snow is getting heavier.

But nothing's going to stop me now, Danny thinks, pushing ahead into the winter storm. *I've had every element thrown at me, and I've survived it all: fire, water, air—now earth.*

And it feels now like he's running on some new energy—not the repeatedly tapped reserves of adrenaline, anger, fear—just a growing certainty, deep in his soul, that the end is approaching. Like that feeling toward the finale of one of the Mysterium's shows. Everything building—risk, excitement, the music—all approaching that moment of release when the last chord burst and died and the lights went up and the company linked hands and stood acknowledging the applause—exhausted, elated, relieved.

Momentum. All the tension that's been cranked into the mechanism now running to its conclusion.

Max stumbles. His hand leaves a red smudge on the snow. He tightens the grubby cloth around it with his other hand.

"You should get to a hospital," Danny shouts. He doesn't want to lose his new companion, but the wound looks pretty bad, and he's worried Max will slow him down.

Max shakes his head. "It's OK," he says. "Alekans aren't quitters, Danny. I can keep going. We need some transport and I can translate if necessary."

They struggle on down the block of Communist-era buildings, past a massive spray-painted image of an astronaut floating in a sea of psychedelic colors, past a padlocked and silent storage unit. Rounding a corner they find themselves on a bigger road and, not far off, see the yellow headlights of a car struggling down the main road.

Max flies for it, his boots kicking up the snow, and virtually throws himself onto the car's hood.

Danny joins him to find the elderly driver in quick-fire discussion with his injured friend.

"It's OK," Max says. "We're on our way. This kind man will help."

Danny clambers into the back, making room at his feet for Herzog. "Can we borrow a phone?"

"No point. Seems the network's down. Has been for half an hour."

25

WHEN ETERNITY BECKONS

It was always Dad's contention that life was about timing.

Not just whether you got the curtain up on time, covered the road to the next city by the appointed hour, got the card you needed to the top of the pack before the reveal of the trick—but far more.

It was a matter of joy and humor: building expectation to just the right note before firing a thunder flash—or dropping the fake snow from the hemisphere.

It was a matter of beauty: if the band was in perfect time with the performers, then that last great crash of guitar coincided exactly with the swan dive from the trapeze, the splash of a cymbal emphasizing a dramatically thrown hand of triumph—and the audience felt their heart lift.

And it was a matter of life and death: one split second too late and the acrobat you were supposed to be catching was on his or her way to the net below or worse. The slightest delay in correcting your position and you were off the wire and falling. A news story.

That's all well and good, Danny thinks, leaning forward from the backseat of the car, feeling the vehicle lurch on the treacherous road surface. But you can only get the timing right if you're in control of all the surrounding factors, if you've rehearsed, if you're doing something you've done a thousand times before.

But now everything is conspiring against even an attempt at timing. It's *all* improvisation—has been ever since the bomb ripped a chunk of his boarding school apart—just a matter of making things up on the spot and hoping for the best. And now, there are just too many unknowns: no way of knowing where Darko is, no way of contacting the others, no idea how long this car ride will take.

In the front seat Max is keeping up a running discussion in German with the elderly driver, pointing ahead with his good arm, the windshield wipers fighting to keep their vision clear. They're on an overpass across the railway lines now, but progress seems pitifully slow. Danny's fists are loosely bunched and he drums them impatiently on his knees. Max leans round. "It's plowed up ahead. We'll only be a few minutes. Don't worry."

Laura crosses the square in front of the Reichstag, her canvas shoes filling with slushy snow, the ridiculous flap-eared hat jammed down on her head. For the umpteenth time she glances at her mobile. Still no sign of a blasted signal!

Through the snow she can see a big top, another beyond it—and then, yes!—the familiar swell of the dark blue Mysterium. *When I get hold of that boy,* she thinks, *I'm going to give him a piece of my mind, give him a big hug—and then not let him out of my sight until we're somewhere very safe indeed.*

Darko is ready to rehearse. He looks away toward Billy and Maria. "Music when you're ready, please," he booms.

The Wheel of Life stands in the center of the performance space, and its colors sparkle in the spotlights. High overhead the tent pushes against the weather outside—just the slightest shiver to give away the gusting wind. But inside everything is still.

"Remember, Sing Sing," he says, "we won't spin fast and if you want to stop at any point just shout. Otherwise it'll be just like the other day." Sing Sing nods solemnly. "I'm ready."

She climbs into place on the footposts, spreading out her arms and taking careful grip of the hand straps. Quietly, under her breath, she's whispering encouragement to herself. "No problem. No flipping problem . . ." *Danny will be proud,* she thinks. *Need to look brave for him. As brave as he's been. As brave as Lily—Mum—was . . .*

She looks up to where the tent fabric curves up out of sight into the dark air above, composing herself.

"I won't do anything fancy," Darko calls. "Just simple throws, no behind the backs. I want to get this right."

"I should hope so!" Zamora coughs. *Is there something odd about Darko?* he thinks. *Something tightening him up a bit more than usual?* Probably just the cold. Or the extra care he's taking with Sing Sing.

Zamora looks around, trying to ignore the insistent ache in his arm. The others are keeping a respectful hush as Darko warms his throwing arm, Aki and Bea huddled together, a blanket around their shoulders. *Thought there was something going on there. Ah, young love,* he thinks, remembering last night's call to Gala with a warm glow. *Nice to be back in touch after so long . . .*

Rosa comes over and puts an arm around his shoulder. "OK, my old friend? We'll get you back in the action again soon!"

Zamora nods. Joey and Bjorn are running through a checklist and sorting equipment into neat piles. Frankie's at the mixing desk, Billy strapping on his guitar, Maria poised at the mic and gripping her drumsticks, ready to accompany Darko. Where have Danny and Laura got to anyway? The lad will want to see this.

"Cue music," Darko calls. "Remember, Sing Sing—jump after you feel knife eight."

He nods to Billy and Maria and a jumpy, clattering rhythm erupts from the sound system. Insistent drumbeat, hacksaw guitar, and then Maria's raw voice punching through it.

"Here's a story about a girl . . ."

Darko presses a pedal with his foot and the wheel—Buddhas, clouds, and Sing Sing—slowly start to spin.

The first knife is in his hands, and he takes a half step forward as the sound of the guitar rips the air, and Maria hisses out the words: "Her bad dreams were just like mine . . ."

Uneasy, Zamora moves closer. He's never liked this routine much. The kind of stereotyping they're meant to get away from in a "new" circus outfit like this.

That's why I'm glad to be clear of that stupid cannon, he thinks. *I can be what I want to be. An artist, a strongman—who just happens to be a bit shorter than most people. Would be better if we mixed it up—put one of the guys on the board maybe, rather than a damsel in distress . . .*

But Rosa says it's a crowd pleaser. Gives people a sense of real danger, and the way Darko does it feels like a twist on the traditional versions. And Sing Sing seemed keen as anything. Trying to prove herself probably.

A searing burst of music, and Darko's hand flashes—a white streak in the gloom: the first knife has struck, quivering just to the side of Sing Sing's right leg. As she and the board cartwheel on the spot, Maria whispers the first chorus in a sudden lull of the guitar: "*. . . from here . . . to . . . infinity . . . from here . . . tooooooo . . . infinityyyy . . .*"

Darko picks the next knife, adjusts his position, flings again. Then another. Above the thumping music you can hear the blows thud into the board.

A tap on the shoulder then makes Zamora jump, and he wheels round to see Laura, her familiar face framed by the borrowed hat, doing her best to smile at him. She's struggling to get her breath back. "Miss Laura! How good to see you!"

Laura pats him on the good shoulder. "What happened to you?"

"Long, stupid story," Zamora shouts over the music.

Laura peers past him, her eyes sparking first in disbelief—then recognition. "Who's that on the wheel? My God, is that Sing Sing?'

Zamora nods. Another knife goes hurtling across the gap between Darko and his target. *Thunk.*

"She looks just like Lily up there . . ." Laura mouths in amazement.

"I know. Spooky, huh?" Zamora shouts, looking around. "So where's Danny?"

"What do you mean *where's Danny*?" Laura's eyes widen in alarm.

"Darko said you were with him—" The words stall in Zamora's throat. It feels like something's just slipped in his mind. Something's wrong, but he can't work out what it is.

The music's still clattering loudly, Maria pummeling her standing drums. Darko's bending for the next knife. He presses the foot switch again. The wheel spinning faster than before: *"From here . . . to . . . eternity . . ."*

"Hey, Darko!" Zamora booms, jogging forward. "Darko! Where did you say Danny is?"

The knife thrower looks up sharply, a blade bright in his hand, an odd expression creasing his face.

And then Danny bursts through the curtain, running full speed toward Darko.

"Stop! STOP! Darko!"

The knife thrower turns away from the board— and a look of astonishment freezes his features for a moment. Then he raises his throwing arm, the knife poised, glittering in his hand.

But Zamora has already read his intentions. The look in Darko's face as he spins toward Danny—the ragged anger spreading across it—says everything that needs to be said.

"NO!" Zamora bellows and sprints forward.

Danny's own footsteps falter as Darko turns toward him. The knife thrower looks him right in the eyes—and then hurls the blade with all his strength.

A blur in front of Danny's eyes, something blocking his vision. There's a grunt, a muffled cry—and Zamora falls to the ground, spinning over onto his back to reveal the blade sticking from his chest.

The music clatters to a stop, Billy's guitar squealing feedback, then cutting dead. For a second nobody moves. Zamora rolls onto his side, groaning in the sudden silence. The wheel's still spinning, but it's slowing, losing momentum and coming to a stop. Sing Sing's face is disorientated, then horror-struck, as she takes in what's happened.

Danny looks from the prone form of Zamora to Darko's empty hand and back again. And then, with a roar, he hurls himself toward the knife thrower.

Darko grabs another blade and flings it, but Danny's ready now and dodges it neatly. Seeing the others running toward him, Darko grabs the last knife, swivels on the spot and makes a dash for the emergency exit.

Bjorn has reacted the fastest of all and is racing along the ringside, closing off the knife thrower's escape. "Come on then!" he yells. "Just try me, Darko!"

"Never liked you Klowns," Darko hisses and flicks his hand, sending the knife spinning. Bjorn sees it late, ducks, but it strikes his shoulder and he grunts in pain. His stride falters and Darko is away, under the glowing green Exit sign, silhouetted for a moment in the doorway—and then gone.

Behind, Danny is crouched over his friend.

There's blood flowing from the wound. "Major? Major? Are you OK?"

Zamora's face is pinched in pain, but then it seems to soften a bit.

"Call an ambulance," Rosa is shouting. "Maria! First aid!"

Danny leans in close, putting his arm around Zamora's shoulder.

"It's OK, Mister Danny," Zamora grunts. "It's not that deep . . . I'll be OK. As long as he didn't get you . . ."

Sing Sing staggers from the target board, steadying herself against the dizziness, moving toward them uncertainly.

"Let's get him, Danny," she snarls. "Let's catch Darko before he disappears."

Danny glances back down at Zamora. The Major nods at him, his eyes half closed, as Maria presses a dressing to the wound and holds it there with shaking hands.

"Go on—guess I'm heading back to the hospital . . ."

Danny bites his lip hard, unable to decide for a moment. "I'll be back in a few minutes."

Zamora nods, smiles through the pain, and gives a thumbs-up. "I'm a rock, remember. The rock of the Mysterium, no?"

Danny hesitates another heartbeat or two and then jumps to his feet and charges for the exit, with Sing Sing close behind.

"No! For God's sake, no!" Laura shouts. "Stay here!" But seeing they're paying her no attention, she scrambles to follow.

Zamora lies back down, closing his eyes. The pain's not so bad now. The knife really hurt when it hit, but it's easing now. He feels OK. Really OK. A warmth coming back into his body and a sense of light and ease. He lets out another breath and a strange, but familiar, well-being floods through him.

When he opens his eyes again he's sitting on the pine needles on that little Swedish island, looking around at the light on the lake, listening to the soft lapping of the waves on the beach. And the sun's shining and there's a waft of food and smoke from the campfire. Everything—yes, everything—is so very calm . . .

26

WHEN EVERYTHING IS BLACK AND WHITE

Outside, the wind has died. Night is falling with the snowflakes and the world is suddenly still. Darko has about a two-hundred-foot head start. He's struggling through the fresh snow, glancing back, making for his camper van, a black figure in a white landscape.

Danny and Sing Sing sprint after him as fast as they can, Danny trying to tell himself that Zamora will be fine while Sing Sing screams at the top of her lungs: "We're gonna get you, Darko! You're a dead man!"

At that moment Max appears from around the side of the camper, his damaged hand still clutched to his chest, the other brandishing one of the giant tent spikes. His eyes are shining as he makes a dash for the knife thrower.

Darko veers away, dodging under the impending blow, and the momentum sends Max sprawling, the spike crunching into the snow. Darko hesitates now. Aki has covered the ground from the tent and is blocking the route to the camper. The knife thrower weighs up his options and then darts away toward the road that runs along the River Spree.

"Don't let him get away," Sing Sing shouts, but Danny's already outrunning her, closing the gap to Darko across the frozen ground.

"Wait for me," Laura calls, stumbling behind. "Wait for me!"

Ahead there's a rumble of engines.

From round the bend in the road comes a string of three rattly old Trabant cars—one zebra striped, one sky blue, one hot pink—the last guided Trabi safari of the day, puffing out exhaust as they rumble toward the Brandenburg Gate and home.

Darko dashes straight in front of the lead car, gesticulating wildly at the driver who brakes in alarm. The Trabant skids to a stop on the icy surface. In a flash, Darko pulls the door open and throws the startled man from the vehicle with incredible force, before jumping into the driver's seat. He revs the engine fiercely and plows away, wheels spinning up snow, the back fishtailing as he goes.

The other two cars have come to a stop, their passengers scrambling out to help the dazed driver from the first Trabi.

Sing Sing has caught Danny now—and they exchange a nod before covering the last of the ground to the idling blue car.

"I'm driving," Sing Sing grunts, throwing herself behind the wheel.

Ahead, Darko's cornering hard to the right. Danny jumps into the passenger seat, eyes straining to keep sight of the zebra stripes as they flash behind the trees, and his sister crunches the gears and urges her Trabi forward.

"Wait!" Laura's voice is lost amongst the angry shouts from the original occupants of the cars.

"What kind of car is this?" Sing Sing grimaces, accelerating hard, fighting the wheel as the car vibrates around them.

"Trabant. Used to be the only kind of car in the East."

"Well, hold on! I've never driven on snow . . ."

"You can do it," Danny shouts over the engine. He glances in the rearview mirror and sees Laura, Aki, and Max piling into the pink car, shoving the other safari guests out of the way. "Darko's the Center," he says quietly. "He must have killed Mum and Dad."

"I kind of got that," Sing Sing shouts.

As they accelerate, Danny suddenly remembers that photograph of Javier's—the one with the whole company and that mysterious figure in the doorway. Like a premonition: Darko, of course, hovering, watching—his actions hard to read. And then all that misdirection and suggestion: look here, don't look here. Throwing everyone off the scent by killing La Loca when too many people were on hand to witness things.

But why not let me fall from the crane then? Maybe my grip was just too firm to shake—?

"Oi, Danny!" Sing Sing shouts. "Any idea where he's going?"

They're racing past the Brandenburg Gate now, the zebra Trabi swerving round a snowplow, overtaking it, carving away along the old line of the old Wall.

"No idea. But he's running. We've got the initiative at last. We can't lose him . . ."

Their car shudders then, and Sing Sing's hands flash on the wheel, trying to correct the spin. Her feet stomp up and down on the pedals, but the skid already has momentum and they sweep through a full 360 degrees, rocking to a stop against the snow-packed curb.

"OK. Getting the hang of it now," she grunts, and shifts the car forward again.

"Can you catch him?"

"'Course I can."

The Tiergarten is a dark smudge to their right, and now—to the left—they're passing a vast field of black square stones, each topped with snow, the paths between them sinking ominously into shadow. Like tombstones or something.

Danny fixes his eyes back on their target. At least the traffic's light on this street, and it's easy to pick out the Trabi's distinctive paint job. And Sing Sing is indeed getting the hang of the ancient vehicle, squinting into the half-light, feeding petrol to the engine, tapping the brake carefully and only when she needs to.

Vast modern buildings rear up to their right now, polished steel and glass reflecting the chase as Darko thumps through a red light, then slides a long turn into Leipziger-Strasse.

"Hold on!" Sing Sing mutters, and wobbling on the treacherous surface, throws them into his tracks, dodging an oncoming bus—and suddenly they're right behind Darko.

Behind, shaken and blurred, Danny can see the pink Trabi bump around the same corner. It veers up onto the pavement, clips the railings to the U-Bahn, then bangs back down onto the street. Looks like Laura's driving and Max is in the front passenger seat. Reassuring to have someone else with them! After all, what hope do they have if they don't catch Darko before he joins the rest of the Forty-Nine? Two children against—what?—an army? If only the Major was here with them now . . .

He'll be OK, Danny thinks, trying to convince himself. *He gave me the thumbs-up, just like he always did at the end of a cannonball flight. Just have to catch Darko. Nail him. Then tell Zamora about it later. He'll enjoy hearing about this ridiculous chase. We'll laugh about it. I just shouldn't have been so hard on him back in Barcelona, about his misjudgment of Javier. Everyone makes errors. Jugglers drop things, acrobats fall.*

The car shudders, its engine grinding.

"Do these things always sound this bad?" Sing Sing shouts. "Sounds like it's coming to bits."

The zebra Trabi turns right abruptly, but Darko's misjudged things a bit and his car bodychecks a wall, before bouncing back off it, regaining the road with an uncertain shiver. And with Sing Sing cutting a perfect corner, they close the gap right up behind his belching exhaust pipe.

"We've got him! We've got him!" Sing Sing yelps, her eyes shining. She thumps her foot to the floor, wiggles left, and accelerates alongside the black-and-white striped car. But they're approaching a T-intersection at speed now, a long, gray stretch of surviving Wall blocking the route ahead.

"Put your seatbelt on!" Sing Sing shouts, grappling to fit hers one-handed.

"What are you going to do?" Danny says.

"Ram him, of course."

For a second or two, Danny is right alongside Darko. The knife thrower looks straight at him—a look so furious, so intense that it jars through him—and then, *wham*, Sing Sing pulls the wheel over hard and strikes car against car. Darko's face tightens and then he swings his Trabi violently back at them.

Sing Sing stomps on the brake but too hard, and their car is skidding again. Darko's Trabi catches them a crunching blow to the front right bumper—so hard that it sends them spinning, wildly out of control. "Brace!" Sing Sing shouts, but Danny's already covered his head with his arms, feet planted on the shaking floor of the car. A ping from the suspension as they thump sideways up the curb and then they bang against the Wall, jerked in their seats like marionettes as they rock back from the impact.

The car will be done for, Danny thinks, preparing to jump out—to stop the others in the pink Trabi as they pass. But the engine, at least, is made of sterner stuff. It's still rumbling steadily, and with a ripping of metal, a bumper tearing loose, Sing Sing has them away again just as Laura, Aki, and Max hurtle past.

"Nobody flipping overtakes me," Sing Sing growls and they lurch forward again. "Checkpoint ahead!"

A few tourists are still out and braving the weather. They look on with astonishment now, as first one ancient car, then another, then a third, hurtles down the street, crossing the old border from West to East, all within feet of one another, all going far too fast, each on the verge of losing control. Two policemen in a stationary squad car on a side road watch them pass—and then the passenger grabs for her radio.

Expertly—possibly recklessly—Sing Sing overtakes the pink car and aims their hood straight at

Darko's exhaust. As they swerve back onto Leipziger-Strasse, the gap's closed right down again.

"Just keep on his tail. Don't ram him again," Danny says, trying to keep his voice steady as the Trabi rattles and rolls into the east side of the city.

The lying snow is worse again here. Darko's car churns through a couple of small drifts, and—for a second—it looks as though he will be caught in one of them. Danny unbuckles his belt, readying himself to bail out, cover the ground, get a grip on this man who has suddenly transformed from company member and lifelong friend to nightmare figure. *He put a knife in Zamora*, Danny repeats to himself. *So you should be ready to do anything to stop him. He killed Mum and Dad, remember that, he killed them . . .*

But the car shakes itself free and is away again. Danny glances at Sing Sing as she lines their Trabi up in Darko's tracks. "He was responsible for the fire, Sing Sing. He killed them."

"He'll pay for it, Danny."

There's a look now in her face—so dark and raw that it's unsettling. A glimpse of her life among the underworld in Hong Kong, the things she's seen there.

The Trabis tear on into the evening, cutting along

the river and then over it toward the tower blocks of Friedrichshain as darkness settles on the city.

Trailing by a couple of minutes, two unmarked white vans with tall, quivering radio antennae race in pursuit. And, a minute behind that, a police car going full pelt spins its blue lights against the snow.

Ahead of them all, like a cloudy blue marble, the Die Welt balloon is descending after its last flight of the day, sinking back into the skyline of East Berlin, its frozen passengers getting ready to disembark and seek warmth.

————————————

And, way back in the Tiergarten, Zamora lies back on the soft, warm bed of pine needles, the sun on his face and the water lap, lap, lapping on the beach of that distant, peaceful island.

27

WHEN GRAFFITI MATTERS

The city looks rougher here, bleak in the failing light, the ravages of the last century still not completely swept away.

Their Trabi is hesitant now and it feels like it's suffered more than a bent bumper with the ramming of the Wall. Darko has reopened the gap, and Danny's body is tensing up, willing the car to keep going. The engine coughs hard, and spasms rack through the thin bodywork, a grinding noise filling the cramped interior.

"What's happening?"

Sing Sing frowns, waggling the steering wheel. "I think the steering column's just gone. Look!" She hauls the wheel over—and nothing happens, just a slow drift across the road the other way, straight toward an oncoming snowplow, shredding its orange lights across the snow.

The plow sounds its horn and then brakes hard—just hard enough—and their Trabi drifts past the blade, across the buried pavement, before jarring to a stop in a cluster of rubbish bins.

Sing Sing breathes out hard and switches off the engine, then swivels in her seat looking for Laura and the third car.

"We're gonna need to hitchhike, Brother."

But Danny's eyes are scouring the park ahead, his eyes caught by a sudden movement. There's a line of trees in front of them, and beyond, a park of some kind, its ground rising and falling in snowy waves, wide and empty. Then he sees the car.

"I can see, Darko!"

Through the trees he can just make out the strobing of the zebra Trabi. Darko's cutting away from the road, bumping through the snow, his headlights shimmying on the undulating ground. Their feeble beams pick out a solitary building—some kind of tower—and Darko brings the Trabi to a stop beside it. Danny scrambles from their stricken car, climbing onto the hood for a better view. The wind has dropped completely now, and in the silence, there's the distinct sound of a car door slamming—and there's Darko himself! A quick glimpse of his black form crossing the snow to the tower and then he vanishes into the shadows at the building's base.

"We've got him," Danny says.

"What do you mean?"

"We've run him to ground."

The pink Trabi rumbles up to the curb, Max leaning out of the window in the front passenger seat. "You're OK?"

Danny points ahead through the trees. "There's a tower or something there. He went into it."

Max squints through the snow. "It's an old watchtower. Part of the Wall system. We're back on the old border here."

"What's in the tower?"

"Nothing. Almost all of them have been pulled down. Probably a guardroom below—and then the viewing platform."

"Why would he go in there?" Laura says, getting out of the car, staring in the direction Danny's pointing.

"Doesn't matter," Danny says. "If he's in there, then he's trapped." Without waiting for the others, he jumps down from the hood and is away across the snow. He covers the ground as fast as he can, feet sinking in the deeper drifts, then through the trees. On their far edge he pauses.

The tower stands on its own, its darkened observation windows watching silently over the parkland. Not a hint of light or life to be seen in them. Below, the building's concrete walls are covered with a mess of graffiti tags and images, plastered one over the other in chunks of blood red, lemon yellow, ice blue. Cut into the wall is a small door, firmly shut.

Nothing else to see. Certainly no hint of a legion of heavily armed criminals. No gun barrels pointing from the windows. *But we'd be easy targets on the open ground*, Danny thinks. Beyond the tower restless crows are trying to settle for the night, flapping out of the tangle of trees and back down again, calling darkly.

The others rush to join him. Aki pats Danny on the shoulder, looking ahead intently. "We're a company, remember? Let's keep together." Sing Sing is already taking a few hesitant steps out into the open.

"What do you think?" Laura says, turning to Max.

"Let's rush him. Five of us—"

"Four and a half," Laura says nodding at his hand. "And we don't have a single weapon among us."

"I don't think he's got a gun," Danny says, turning to follow his sister. "And we've got Sing Sing . . ."

They cross the ground quickly, half crouched, senses primed, ready for the crack of a bullet, the stutter of something heavier.

But nothing comes. The tower stands before them, brooding and silent. A tall, bare flagpole sticks clear of it, glinting in the reflected car headlights. Still no sound from inside—just the *caw caw* of the crows as they come back down into roost. And maybe a siren half a mile or so away, filtering through the steady snowfall.

They cover the last few paces at a sprint, relieved to be up against the wall of the tower. Aki tugs sharply at the door handle, but it won't budge.

"Open the door, Darko!" Laura shouts. "We've got you cornered. And the police are with us . . ." She glances over her shoulder uncertainly, in the direction of the siren.

No answer.

"Open this door, you lowlife!" Sing Sing shrieks, kicking the door hard, the resounding metal clang sending the crows clattering up into the air again. "Or I'll kick it off its hinges!"

But Danny's attention has switched, his eyes

fastening to something. Amidst the clutter of graffiti tags, band names, leering faces—tucked in amongst the spray-painted neon colors—is something he's almost expected to find. Something that tightens his breathing, sending a bump of nervous energy into his system: a neat grid of seven-by-seven black dots, very small, but perfectly done on a white square painted directly over the lintel of the door.

And a red circle stamped around the very middle point.

You'd miss it if you weren't looking for it. And even if you saw it nobody would know what it was . . .

He looks up and catches a sudden flicker of movement. Fastened just under the roof, a small security camera is rotating toward them, its red light blinking steadily.

"I think this might be more than just a hiding place," he says quietly and points at the grid over their heads.

Laura takes in a sharp breath. "But there can't be much in there. And I can't hear anything. Are you sure he went in?"

"Yes. I'm sure. And there are no tracks leading away from it."

Sing Sing turns back to him impatiently. "Danny, pick this flipping lock and let's get that rat."

Danny nods. The quicker the better. This final confrontation needs to happen, as quickly as possible—and then they can hurry back to Zamora. But he has a growing sense of unease. That little grid—the dots that have haunted his every step from cold England to steaming Hong Kong, from the vibrancy of Barcelona to this graffiti-covered remnant of the Cold War—that grid, with its little circle around the central dot, says one thing: he's reached the target.

Dead center.

Fingers twitching with the cold, the anticipation, he bends to peer at the lock, his hand resting on its icy metal handle, trying to look confident, braver than he feels.

"I'll have a go," he says. "But we might need a bit more help . . ."

And then the lock gives a faint click, and slowly, silently, the door swings open.

28

WHEN TO USE
ACROBATICS TO BEST
ADVANTAGE

"Darko?" Danny calls.

His voice dies on the cold, damp air inside. Nothing coming back, except that peculiar empty feeling that empty buildings generate. The sixth sense that there's nobody home.

"Come out! Hands high!" Max growls. Still nothing.

Sing Sing pushes past the others, crouching. "Come on then, scumbag! You should have skewered me when you had the chance."

Danny follows her into the windowless ground-floor space.

"Careful," Laura hisses, "he may still be armed."

"Can't see a thing," Aki mutters. He pulls his mobile from his pocket and glances at it. "Still no signal, but we can use this."

He holds the phone up high, the dull green glow from its display picking out shapes now: an old table, some benches. Graffiti on the inside of the walls—goggle-eyed, gas-masked figures, spiky words. *Capitalism destroys!*

Aki nudges Danny. At the far side a steep ladder climbs clear of the guardroom and disappears through a hatch into the gloom above.

"He's got to be up there," Aki says. "He could pick us off one by one as we go up."

"Any ideas?" Laura says, moving to the bottom of the rungs, looking up uncertainly.

"I don't think he's there," Danny says.

Max is still standing in the doorway, looking back to where the sirens are swelling in the distance. "What did you say?"

"He's not up there. I just know it."

"So where is he then, Brother?" Sing Sing says impatiently. "Don't give me that mysterious voice stuff."

Danny shakes his head. "Maybe there's another door . . . Look, I'll show you . . ."

He grabs the handrail and climbs quickly, surely—just like going up the ladder to the high wire.

There's a trapdoor shut across the top, but it's not locked and he bangs up through it, throwing caution to the wind, eager to rule out this dead end. *What if I'm wrong?* he thinks at the last minute as he pushes through it. *What if he just stabs me as I come through . . .*

But, as he thought, there's no one there. Misdirection again—the magician always makes you think you know where the coin is, but he's already managed to get it somewhere you wouldn't guess.

Windows on three sides of the observation floor throw faint light onto the rubbish-strewn floor. Through them Danny can see the undulating snowy ground where the Wall once ran, the trees, the distant blocks of Kreuzberg. A hint of flickering blue light beyond.

No sign of a dark figure hurrying away. No fresh tracks in the snow as far as he can see.

It all looks so still. A moment of quiet and balance, like that point on the trapeze when acrobats reach the top of their swing and seem to hang for that precious, weightless second. Beauty and danger inextricably bound.

The snow's getting heavier again—falling straight down, steadily, as if this is the start of a seriously long night of snow. That movement, down, down, down, holds his gaze again for a long half minute. Everything falls in the end—

"Danny?" Sing Sing's head has popped through the hatch. "What's going on?"

"He's not here."

"But he can't just have disappeared."

"I grew up in the Mysterium," Danny says, with a grim smile. "Anything's possible!"

They both drop quickly back down the ladder to the floor below.

"And . . . ?" Max says, stepping back in.

Sing Sing shrugs. "Not a sign."

There's an electrical buzz then above their heads, and a striplight blinks into hesitant life.

"Good stuff, Max," Laura mutters. "Where was the switch?"

"It wasn't me—" Max starts to say, but he's cut short as the door behind him slams shut. It's followed by the sharp snap of a bolt slotting home.

"What's going on?" Max groans, tugging hard at the door. "Locked. Must have been someone outside."

A stark light is flooding the guardroom now.

At least that might shine out from the windows above, Danny thinks. *Like a kind of lighthouse—it might guide someone in to help us. Maybe those sirens are coming our way.*

But then the trapdoor above booms shut and locks. The sounds resonate in the concrete echo chamber of the guardroom as they all look around bewildered.

"Got to be some kind of remote control," Laura says. "Looks like we're trapped."

"Maybe Darko just wants to keep us locked up until the heist is done," Sing Sing says. "What do you think, Brother?"

"I don't know." He scans the room quickly and his eyes fix on a shiny metal pole in the corner. It rises from a hole in the concrete floor and sticks up the full height of the room, before disappearing into the viewing gallery above.

"I thought there was a flagpole sticking up from the roof," he says, pointing at it. "But it must have been this—it must be a radio mast."

Max has already joined him and looks up to where the pole disappears. "Got to be the transmitter," he says. "They must be blasting the signal out from here." He looks down at his feet, to where the mast cuts down into the concrete. "Everyone spread out and check the floor. He must be beneath us."

The door's easy to find now: like any trick it's obvious once you know the secret—and this is nothing more sophisticated than the old hidden trapdoor. Under the guardroom table, there's a neatly cut section of floor with less than an inch of gap framing it. No sign of a handle or ring to pull, though.

"It's got to be opened from inside," Danny says. "Which means there's at least one other person down there, right?"

"Probably a whole lot more," Max says quietly. He goes over and stands on the trapdoor, then stamps on it. "I think we're standing on the vipers' nest."

A grinding starts beneath his feet—a mechanism firing—and he stumbles to one side as the trapdoor tips up, pushed by a well-greased hydraulic arm.

Another vertical ladder leads down into the darkness.

"I think we're being invited to join them," Laura says, wrinkling up her face. "What do you think, Max?"

"I think we're in trouble." He cocks his head, listening intently to the silence. "Maybe we should wait and see if the police are coming. I'm sure those sirens are getting closer."

But Danny's waited long enough for this moment. He needs to know everything now. To see what lies at the heart of the grid of dots.

He takes a breath—and starts down the ladder.

Cold emanates from the walls as he descends ten, fifteen, twenty feet. No sound but his own feet soft on the metal rungs, the heavier tread of Aki and Laura above his head.

He's remembering the action films he used to watch with Dad—those perilous journeys to the lair of the supervillain. Gleaming control rooms, flying balconies, banks of computer screens and illuminated maps. Is that what waits for them? Darko sitting in some wing-backed chair, spinning round, his fingers steepled thoughtfully . . .?

But the truth is far less glamorous.

The ladder drops into a long metal box of a room, dank and echoey.

Max comes down last, struggling one-handed on the ladder. He takes a quick look round at the silent, ribbed chamber, ghostly in the light from Aki's smartphone.

"Shipping unit," he says. "Like on the big cargo boats. I've seen this kind of thing in Sicily, with the Mafia. They bribe construction workers and then sink these into the ground, join them up. They must have done it ages ago, though—when they were knocking down the Wall here to make the park."

"Maybe it joins some of the old tunnels under this part," Laura says. "The escape tunnels that people tried to dig."

"We'll have to write this story together, *schatzi*," Max says, forcing a smile. "Pool our knowledge."

Laura puffs the hair from her eyes. "As long as I get top credit!"

"There's a door here," Danny says impatiently.

This one's more like a porthole: a round hatch like you'd find below decks on a submarine. It swings open to reveal a tunnel, and Danny clambers through, into some kind of utility piping—smooth, black plastic—that runs gently down for thirty feet or so. It deposits him in a second, empty shipping container.

Another door at the far end. He's moving fast now, momentum carrying him forward to see what lies beyond. Without waiting for the others, crouching, he drops down another length of sloping pipeway, toward dim light ahead, his hands braced against the smooth sides of the corridor.

This pipe bends sharply to the right and the light gets brighter. And now, over the shuffle of his feet, the thudding of his heart, he can hear a hubbub of voices thickening the air—the way an audience murmurs before the lights drop, before you're suddenly onstage, bright and spotlit. *Need to make a bold entrance*, he thinks. *Everything can depend on that first moment as you make your appearance.* He turns another corner, drops a short flight of metal steps—and finds himself confronted by a roomful of people.

As one, the men and women of the Forty-Nine turn to stare at him—and the room falls silent.

They're gathered around a large trestle table—some on their feet, some sitting in plastic garden chairs. But instead of the eager, supportive faces of an audience, each set of eyes shows anger, hostility, the threat of violence. Kwan sits amongst them—his face, at least, registering something else. Astonishment. Fear maybe? *After all,* Danny thinks, *he's twice seen me rise from the dead.*

On the far side of the table, chin resting on his hand, Darko is looking straight at him. He's trying to appear calm, Danny realizes, but the effort of the chase through the snow is still pushing at his shoulders. And something more is playing on his face: a sense of urgency, anxiety.

"Bravo! Welcome to Forty-Nine HQ," Darko says. "Not even your dad worked out where this was." Danny stands firmly in the doorway and waits.

Nothing can ever match that overwhelming terror at the bottom of the grave—and there's just a shred of hope forming at the back of his mind now. *I've come this far and I'm still walking*, he thinks. *There'll be a way—just one more lock to crack.*

Sing Sing comes clattering into Danny's back and peers silently over his shoulder.

"Got nothing to say?" Darko snaps at them, getting to his feet.

Danny shakes his head and looks around. This is no film set. Just a large concrete chamber with pipes and grubby wires strung along the walls. Some electrical equipment is stacked in the corner—router cables and power leads tangled like cooked spaghetti, running up onto the massive table strewn with laptops, maps, pizza and burger boxes, beer cans. The backs of the white plastic chairs are each marked with a number—and that grid again, a different red dot on each.

The whole place stinks of sweat and stale food.

Impatiently Darko says, "I've got enough to deal with right now. The weather's messing up our plans and the phone network's down. I haven't got time to see to you, but some of my colleagues will."

Laura is by Danny's side now. She points at Darko, her face a snarl. "People like you should be put away, Blanco. Put away for good—"

"Your brother had it coming. He was responsible for my father's death." Darko's eyes are shining now, intense. "He might as well have pulled the trigger himself. And now I can have revenge and complete the story. We reap what we sow, right? And the rest of the family can die here. All of it."

One of the men at the table looks up sharply from his laptop. "Two vans approaching, Center. I think there are police cars holding off a little way down the street too."

Darko goes over to look at the surveillance images on the screen and pulls a face. "Shut the transmitter down. Told you we've been on the air too long."

"No way out, Darko," Max says firmly. "They've got you."

"Idiot," the knife thrower spits back. "We've got a maze of tunnels behind me. False doors. Deadlocks.

Don't worry about me. Worry about your own soul, Alekan. You and Laura and Danny are the only ones who know the full truth. And it will die with you here."

He looks at the gangsters gathered around the table. They're drawing their weapons, an array of handguns and semiautomatics.

It'll be no contest, Danny thinks. *Unless we can act very quickly. Do something completely unexpected and take the initiative.*

"They're at the door," the man at the monitor says. "They're taking a ram from the back of one of the vans. Armed police there too."

"Close all the sealed doors. Where's the bullion convoy now?" Darko snaps.

"Leaving Tempelhof. Heading toward the city."

A moment of hesitation from the knife thrower. It's all Danny needs.

"Hey, Darko!"

The man looks back at him and their eyes meet. Danny sends everything he's got into that look, his gaze boring into Darko's dark eyes, pushing for a connection. He's got no hope of hypnotizing the man, but just wants to buy a few seconds' distraction, because he's felt that soft nudge of Sing Sing's trainer against his. *Get ready for action*, it says. *Here we go!*

He can feel Aki shifting his position behind him, Sing Sing putting a hand on his shoulder, adjusting her position. *Haven't even got an ace up my sleeve this time*, he thinks ruefully. *Just have to do my best.* He can hear Aki counting down quietly under his breath. "Three . . . two . . ."

"What is it?" Darko says, mockingly opening his own eyes wider. "No time for mentalism, Danny."

"Hup!" Aki shouts loudly, and he launches Sing Sing from his cupped hands. She turns a somersault forward through the air, a perfect flight that lands on strong hands in the middle of the table and then pushes off fast, hurtling feet first toward the knife thrower. Caught by surprise, Darko ducks, but not quickly enough, and he takes a powerful blow to the back of his neck. As he stumbles to the floor the chamber erupts.

Two gunshots detonate in quick succession. Danny races forward and dives under the table.

Looking back he sees Laura duck under the blow aimed at her. She spins along the wall trying to get her balance and—by luck or judgment—thumps the main light switch. Immediately the cellar is plunged into near darkness, lit now only by the glow of the laptops on the table, the electric heaters—and then the ragged bursts of light from the muzzles of ten or more guns. Chaos grips the room. Scrambling under the table Danny bangs into chair legs, ready at any moment for the thudding impact of a bullet or blow, moving fast on all fours toward where Darko fell.

There are cries of pain and alarm overhead. Another stutter of gunfire and the choking bite of smoke fills the air.

"Don't shoot!" someone is screaming.

"Get the lights on!"

"Over here!"

"I'm hit!"

And over that you can hear the familiar hissing of air between Sing Sing's lips as she continues her attack. Laura shouting a warning to Aki.

Another spray of gunfire—and then silence.

Danny is out from under the table now. A laptop slams against the wall over his head, screen shattering, spilling its electronic guts—and he glances back to see Sing Sing kicking wildly, spinning, taking down one, two, three gangsters. Behind her the door bursts open then, and helmeted police fill the doorway, laser sights flashing on the walls, the boom of another gun, returning fire . . .

Where's Darko? Danny looks around.

In the flickering light he's just in time to see the leader of the Forty-Nine roll through a kind of hatch set low in the wall.

It swallows him whole—and then bangs shut.

29

WHEN TO ENTER
THE MAZE

At that moment Sing Sing comes tumbling across the table, thrown by a heavy blow, landing in a jumble of pizza boxes and cans on the floor next to him. Bullets are pinging back and forward in the confined space again. She struggles to get to her feet, but Danny grabs her by the shoulders.

"Keep down, stupid!"

Laura's voice from the far side: "Are you all right, Danny?"

"Yes!" he shouts back through the confusion, trying to keep a hold on his sister. They're trapped on the far side of the room, behind the Forty-Nine.

"Let. Me. Go!" Sing Sing tugs herself free, firing him a fierce look, locked in attack mode.

"Don't be stupid," he snaps. "You'll be shot. I need you. I need your help. Darko got away. Follow me."

As bullets tear the plaster over his head, he crawls to the metal panel in the wall and jabs at it with his foot. It rocks open to reveal a horizontal tunnel leading away into pitch blackness.

"Garbage disposal!" Sing Sing screws her face tight. "Then let's get after him."

The escape route is narrow and runs laterally like an air duct. Sing Sing scrambles in headfirst, and Danny hurries to follow, ducking as her trainers kick forward and threaten to brain him.

Ahead they can hear the fast, frantic pounding of Darko's hands and knees on the metal. Then an abrupt burst of gunfire from behind drowns that out. Danny crawls faster, colliding with Sing Sing, fearing for a moment that someone is firing into the chute. But no ricochet comes bounding down the duct. *It must have been someone firing close to the hatch,* he thinks. There's another enormous bang behind them, and a shock wave rolls past them, making both of them stumble, the noise amplified by the tight walls of the tunnel.

"Faster!" Danny shouts. His voice sounds strangely distant, muffled by the dull ringing in his ears. Must have been a stun grenade. And there's something else now, the whiff of gas seeping down the tunnel, clawing at his nose and eyes, stinging.

There's a thud ahead, and Sing Sing groans.

"Banged my flipping head. Dead end!"

"Can't be!" Danny whispers, straining to listen over the whistling in his ears.

"There's nothing here."

"Wait . . . listen!"

That soft, scurrying sound again, but now it sounds like it's coming from behind them.

"He's behind us!" Sing Sing squeaks. "Turn around!"

"But he can't have got past!"

Danny contorts his body, turning back on himself, squinting back down the chute. There's a tiny rectangle of dim light in the distance, where the hatch opens into the control room, but nothing moving between here and there. Then—with a sudden *thunk*—that last bit of light is snuffed out too, as the door swings shut and they're in complete darkness.

"Now what?" Sing Sing groans.

"Shhh. I can hear him."

Above the high-pitched wobbling in his ears, he can still make out Darko's scuttling retreat.

"So where is he?" Sing Sing moans. "I don't like this . . ."

Danny feels his way carefully back down the chute, hands out to either wall, all his senses open. Darko talked about a maze. And, yes! Here it is, about ten or fifteen feet back, the walls suddenly disappearing on both sides. He spreads his fingers and checks left, then right. Two identical ducts leading away. Which one?

Impossible to tell which is producing the sound—the echoes are too confusing. First, it seems that the right-hand one, then the left is the most likely candidate.

"What is it?" Sing Sing squeaks behind him.

"Shhh! I'm trying to listen. There're two paths."

"We could split up."

"No flipping way."

Sing Sing chokes. "Are you making fun of me?"

"Wait . . ." He senses something else as he bends to this passage on the left, fingers resting lightly on its wall. Tremulous vibrations can be felt there. Faint—but distinct.

"We'll take this one," he says firmly. "Keep close. I don't want to lose you."

"No chance of that. I need to get out of here!"

Danny crawls forward into the new tunnel, going slowly at first, his hands checking the surface, reaching out into the thick darkness to feel for obstacles. There's a metallic bang ahead—some kind of door opening and closing perhaps? Was that a chink of light? Or a trick of his tired eyes, aftereffects of the blow to his head?

"How come he's moving so fast?" Sing Sing says.

"He's fitter than the Klowns. As flexible as the Aerialisques. And he knows where he's going."

"Come on, let's move it!"

Danny hurries ahead. It's horrible really, that blindness, that sense that at any minute you might crawl straight into an obstacle—or something worse.

His hand reaches forward for the next push off the smooth surface and suddenly there's nothing under his hand, his arm sinking into nothing, lurching forward, falling.

A stifled scream comes out of his mouth. He shoots his legs out, bracing hard, and instinctively Sing Sing grabs hold of them with an improvised catcher's grip.

"I've got you," she grunts, "I've got you."

Far below Danny's head—it's impossible to say how far—he can hear running water.

"Pull me back! Quickly!"

He pushes against the smooth duct walls, helping as best he can as Sing Sing hauls him back, breathing hard.

"It's a dead fall. A kind of trap."

"How wide?"

"I don't know. Hold my hand."

He edges forward again, this time finding the lip of the drop with his fingertips, then reaching out across the emptiness, over that fearful depth, as far as his arm can reach—and there it is! Lying on the far side is a loose sheet of metal. With his fingertips he works it back across the void, then gets a good grip, simultaneously lifting and pulling the improvised drawbridge, until it's safely over their side of the chasm. He bangs it down and tests it with a foot.

"Should I go first?"

But Sing Sing is already moving. She pushes past him, barging him out of the way. A kind of electricity is in the air as she squeezes past, her breath coming rapidly in short, shallow breaths.

"I've *got* to get out of here," she says, her voice jumpy now, panicky. She clatters across the makeshift bridge on all fours, firing echoes away down the chute.

At the far side she turns. "Come on, dummy!"

He hurries across to join her, trying not to think of the drop below, hoping the thing is overlapping both sides securely enough. "You need to take a deep breath," he pants. "You're getting upset!"

"'Course I'm flipping upset," Sing Sing. "I hate small spaces. I get claustrophobic and I've done my best to keep it together—and now I've had enough. This is why I gave up contortion!"

They crawl on as fast as they can for another thirty or forty feet, round a corner, and then find themselves against a door. It's locked—but a faint glow is bleeding around the edges. Beyond, not a sound.

"Locked," Sing Sing grunts and then turns in the cramped space, maneuvering her feet to make contact with the blocked door. Danny feels the tension gather in her body—and then she unleashes an explosive kick that rips the hatch straight from its frame.

Seconds later, they're standing in some kind of service corridor, blinking, dazzled by fluorescent light.

Distant footsteps flap away around the corner. They exchange glances and then hurry in pursuit, through double doors, through a storage area of some kind hung with coils of wire and overalls, through a deserted office space, down another long, echoing corridor that leads eventually to a flight of iron steps spiraling up dizzily into the gloom above them.

Still those quick feet can be heard, ringing now on the stairs, gradually being drowned out by a low and ominous rumbling.

"Where are we?" Sing Sing whispers.

"No idea. But we haven't lost him yet."

They start to climb the spiral staircase, two steps at a time, covering ten, twenty, thirty, forty— muscles starting to burn with lactic acid—up and up as the distant roar grows and the steps themselves start to vibrate.

"Sounds like a monster!" Sing Sing shouts.

"We must be at ground level now," Danny pants. "We can't lose him!"

The stairway ends abruptly and they barge through a grilled service door and back into the cold night air. Ahead of them is a freezing, aboveground U-Bahn platform.

The curved station, all scrolling ironwork and bricked arches, is surprisingly busy, raised high above the streets below. Beyond the cover of the roof—out across the river—the snow is falling in thick curtains, veiling the darkness.

Where is he then? Danny thinks. *We can't have lost him. Not now.* The roar of the train approaching from the other direction becomes thunderous and then it thumps around a corner, into the station. Danny's eyes follow the engine as it passes—and, just fifty feet or so away, he sees the unmistakable figure of Darko cutting away through the gaggle of waiting passengers.

30

WHEN TO RISK EVERYTHING

The train doors shudder open and Darko runs straight for the last car. His movements are jerky, hurried, devoid of his usual elegance, as he flings himself aboard.

Did he glance back then?

Danny taps Sing Sing on the shoulder and points. "Front of the train. We need to get closer."

"Did he see us?"

"Don't think so."

Passengers are piling off the U-Bahn, others shuffling to get on—and they're still four cars short when the door alarm sounds.

"Get on," Danny shouts, tugging Sing Sing through the closing doors.

There's an awkward hush in the carriage. Some people are glancing impatiently at their useless smartphones, some gazing out at the falling snow. Sing Sing squints through the window to the next carriage. "What are we going to do?"

Danny looks at the electronic display, then a section of underground map on the wall.

"We're on Line 1. Think we're heading across the river—so there's only one more stop."

"Let's move up the carriages," Sing Sing says. "See if we can get closer?"

"The doors are only for emergencies," Danny says looking at the red sign on the glass.

"I'd call this a flipping emergency, wouldn't you?" Sing Sing says, yanking the door open. People look up in surprise as they rush into the warm bubble of the next car and hurry through it, pushing past the other standing passengers, moving toward the next connecting door.

But then the intercom crackles and the driver's voice fills the carriage—a weary voice full of resignation. Danny tries to understand, but he knows virtually no German and the man's throwing his words out quickly. Something about *schnee*—snow.

". . . entschuldigung, es tut mir leid." The people on the carriage groan as the driver finishes his impromptu speech, turning to the sliding doors or getting to their feet.

Danny turns to an elderly man, who's zipping up his coat with a sigh. "Excuse me, what's going on?"

The man pulls a face. "Too much snow. On the bridge . . ."

The doors are already opening, spilling cold air into the carriages.

"He'll run for it," Danny shouts and fights his way through the other passengers, onto the platform, looking left just in time to see Darko jump from the very last set of doors.

Sing Sing runs to the main station exit. "He can't get out this way! Unless he wants to take me on!"

Danny moves forward against the flow of the departing passengers. For a moment he and the knife thrower have a clear view of each other. Darko's clearly weighing something up, calculating strategy. He glances away over his shoulder, toward the river, out along the elevated rails into the thickly falling snow.

"Stand still!" Danny shouts. "It's all over, Darko!"

He starts to jog toward the familiar figure. The crowd on the platform is thinning, and Darko's moved to stand at the very edge of the platform. He's reaching hurriedly into his pocket now, pulling something out. Danny falters as he tries to see what it is. A last knife? A gun? Surely this vicious man— Center himself—is armed in some way? He's fiddling with something in his hands, shielding it with his body, and then turns suddenly, his arm whipping, launching something into the air.

Danny turns to warn Sing Sing, and as he does so, an explosion rocks the platform, firing back off the station walls. There's a flash, a searing red light burning in the air—and then clouds and clouds of billowing smoke roll across the platform.

It sounds like a bomb going off. Passengers scream, running and scrambling for the exit and the stairs to the street below. But there are no injuries to be seen, no damage to the ornate station, no fallen masonry or bodies.

Just a theatrical thunderflash! Darko must have pinched one from the secure prop box, Danny realizes as he edges forward into the smoke. Figures stumble through the choking cloud—but none of them is the right shape or size for the knife thrower.

The red flare is dying to an ember now. Danny pushes on through the smoke and reaches the edge of the platform—and, of course, there's not a trace of Darko.

Did he slip past in the fog? Danny looks back to see Sing Sing running toward him. "He didn't go down the stairs," she shouts. "And the train's empty. Maybe he crossed the tracks?"

The platform on the other side is deserted. It's less sheltered from the weather, and the snow lies smooth, unbroken on the half closest to the tracks. No footfall there . . .

And now, out of the periphery of his vision, he sees Darko. There to the right! Out on the snowbound tracks, the snaking elevated line curving away into the night toward the river. He's running, stumbling across the snowy railroad ties, rounding the bend, and moving out of sight.

"He's on the tracks!"

Danny races forward, plants a hand in the snow on the platform edge, and hops down onto the tracks, into the yellow glow of the stationary U-Bahn's lights.

"Halt!" the driver shouts. "*Kein Zutritt!*"

"We'll worry about that later," Sing Sing says, pushing past him, jumping to follow her brother.

The man stares in horror after them and then rushes to throw an emergency switch on the wall marked with a lightning bolt.

Danny's already reached the end of the station building. Ahead the tracks curve away, a white pathway leading into the night. The snow is almost thicker than the air now, flakes fluttering against his mouth and eyes, his own feet sinking with each step. Darko's in sight again, about 150 feet ahead, leaning forward into his own effort, stumbling now and then.

"Stop!" Danny shouts. But there's no penetration to his voice now—it's muffled instantly by the engulfing snow.

The elevated stretch of U-Bahn runs out across the river, guarded by thin railings. Glancing down to the right, Danny sees its black water far below, swallowing the millions of snowflakes falling on its surface—as if the river is insatiably devouring the storm.

Darko stumbles again. The gap between them is closing, but then one of his own steps sinks deeper than he's expecting, and he catches the edge of a railroad tie, tripping, throwing out his hands to brace, his face taking the icy slap of the snowdrift.

Sing Sing is with him in a moment holding out her hand. Her face is set, determined. "Get up! We've nearly got him, Brother."

She pulls him to his feet, and they surge on, past a round turret on the bridge, into yet deeper drifts that snag at their legs. It's a slow-motion chase now, all three of them losing strength, stumbling— but they're closing in on Darko, there's no doubt about it.

A second turret materializes from out of the snowy darkness, and they're just ten paces or so behind.

Darko looks back again, then veers left, toward the railing. He throws them a venomous look, plants his hands on the ironwork, and vaults over the side, dropping instantly from sight.

Danny waits for the splash far below. But instead, he hears a dull thump, a groan. Then muffled footsteps racing away.

He dashes to the railing. On this side a road bridge runs below the elevated line. A box van is stuck in the snow, and you can see where Darko has landed in the snow on its roof. A trail of footsteps leads away to where Darko is racing across a patch of waste ground, toward the remnant Wall alongside the river, back toward the East Side Gallery. In the distance, in the parkland beyond that, Danny can see the blue sphere of the Welt balloon tethered for the night.

A siren is wailing not far away . . .

And then a deep boom of thunder breaks and rolls across the city.

31

WHEN YOU GET TO THE TOP . . .

Inspector Jules Ricard is gripping the dashboard of the police cruiser. The vehicle's lights skitter across the white road, reflecting blue off the flakes. He too hears that long drumroll over their head.

He looks up. "What's that?"

The driver raises his eyebrows. "*Schneesturm*. Thunder snow. Didn't see the lightning."

Ricard squints ahead, trying to pick out objects through the storm. "How far now to this watchtower?"

"About a mile. Snow's bad on the Oberbaum Bridge. But we should be OK in this," the driver says, patting the wheel.

On their right the graffitied colors of the

gallery show in the headlights. A large, blue balloon is moored beyond. Ricard glances in the rearview mirror at the convoy of police cars following them. "And it's all under control? They've got it locked down?" Ricard says, tapping the dashboard impatiently.

"It's under control. Three civilians accounted for . . ."

"But the young boy? The girl?"

The man shakes his head. "It's all very confused." Ricard winces. *I can't be too late*, he thinks. *Can't let that boy down. We were probably the last flight into Tegel before they closed that too, so it could be worse. I could be stuck who knows where.*

And then Ricard's jaw drops open and he bangs the driver's shoulder. "Stop! Stop!"

Staggering toward them is a tall figure—and he's being pursued by a familiar, dark-haired boy.

"No!" Ricard shouts. "It's Danny!"

And another movement catches his attention. Running full throttle—along the curved top of the Wall itself—a slim girl . . .

Danny has almost caught up now, getting ready to tackle Darko and hoping that Sing Sing will be close enough to help.

The blue lights ahead are getting closer too— and they're fanning out across the white road and pavement, doors opening even before the vehicles have come to a stop, a loud siren crackling the air. A flash brilliantly lights everything, freeze-framing Darko as he hesitates for a moment. Then the thunder booms overhead and Darko jumps—right into the Wall itself.

Or so it seems. From Danny's point of view it's a magic trick. As if the knife thrower has vanished through solid concrete. But as he covers the last few yards, Danny sees there's a ragged hole in the Wall, the rusting steel bones of its innards exposed to the cold air. He looks through it and sees Darko running away across the rough ground, straight toward the Welt balloon.

"Get him!" Sing Sing screams from overhead.

As Danny scrambles through the hole, she comes hurtling down in a rush of a jump.

"Unggghhh," she grunts, her right leg giving on impact, and then howls as her ankle doubles over. She rolls on the ground, reaching for it with both hands, eyes seeking out Danny in anguish. "Get him," she hisses.

Darko's almost reached the balloon compound now, and Danny sprints away across the snow as fast as he can.

The knife thrower flings himself at the wire link gate, rattling and banging his way over it, then dropping to the far side. He scrambles into the large viewing basket hanging from the blue-white world inflated over his head, hands working fast.

There are shouts, flashing lights behind, but no time to look. Danny plants his fingers in the gaps in the gate, pulling himself up handhold by hand-hold, feet slipping, throwing himself over the top. He lands neatly, then races the last few yards toward the balloon. Just then the balloon's gondola jerks as Darko throws something clear.

Without a sound, the balloon lifts. Very quickly. It's designed only for tethered up-and-down flights, but now without its leash, the helium filled chamber races skyward, as if desperate for its own escape.

With one last effort Danny jumps to grab hold of the metal gondola—missing by a fraction, and the balloon surges up and away. Darko's going to escape! Got to stop him. He looks around wildly and sees a thin rope, snapping in the snow like a writhing snake.

An extra mooring Darko hasn't spotted? A safety line, maybe?

It uncoils rapidly, then snaps tight. There's a cry from the basket, and Danny looks up to see Darko, thirty feet above his head, fumbling at where the line's fastened to the gondola. The balloon still tugging hard to be away.

If you see a rope, climb it. And when you get to the top just keep climbing.

Someone used to say that. Darko himself? *Should I try it? Or just let him go. Get back to Sing Sing. To Zamora.* Now that Center's cover is blown, perhaps the danger is past.

But Danny's body has already made the decision for him. Habit, training, the momentum of the chase all pushing him to climb the taut rope—feet wrapped skillfully, hands firm on the braided line, just like the old days.

He's two-thirds of the way up when tension disappears from the rope as something comes loose below. The line rips free of its connection to the ground—and they're rocketing up into the sky, the ground falling away horribly quickly. Danny looks down. The figures racing to the balloon depot, the spinning police lights, Sing Sing, the Wall, the river shrinking fast . . .

The rope suddenly feels stupidly thin, cold, slippery in his hands. *Keep climbing*, Danny thinks, *it's the only hope now. Just keep putting hand over hand over hand.*

The falling snowflakes seem to be accelerating. The ground blurs, and then they're up and into the cloud. His arms are straining, hands burning—but then he's made it, and he's gripping the steelwork of the gondola, getting a firm hold. And it's not a moment too soon, because Darko's worked his end of the line free, and as Danny transfers his weight to the basket, it suddenly goes tumbling away into the obscuring cloud.

"Should have let me go!" Darko screams from overhead.

Danny looks up, straight into his face. Anything familiar in Darko's features has gone. Just a hostile stare. Rage. A person he doesn't know.

Darko disappears for a second, then is back, some kind of long stick grasped in both hands, a shining metal hook at its end, glinting as the lightning flashes again. He reaches over and starts to thwack at the bottom of the gondola, at Danny's hands.

"This time . . . you're . . . going . . . to fall!" he grunts through gritted teeth.

Danny ducks under the basket, the hook missing his head by inches, then dares to look back again, trying to ignore the drop beneath his feet, his aching arms. This time, the bang of the thunder is so quick, so loud, that it startles even Darko for a second.

And in that second Danny makes his move.

He grabs the end of the stick and pulls himself up—a single movement of such skill, power, and precision that it catches the knife thrower off guard.

Danny perches on the rail of the gondola, dodges under a straight-armed punch from Darko—and he's in the basket.

But in doing that, he loses his grip on the mooring hook, and Darko takes an almighty swing at his head. The metal tip snags Danny's hair—but Darko's missed—and Darko's momentum carries him full speed against the basket edge, and then over it, somersaulting, twisting, grabbing desperately for hold.

He screams. Fear and pain and anger mixed as he hangs by one hand from the rail.

"Help!" Darko shouts. "Danny!"

Danny hesitates.

It's just a tiny fraction of a second—a fraction that he will replay over and over in his mind for years to come. Then he rushes to help, scrambling to the edge of the basket, reaching for Darko's outstretched hand . . .

. . . But he's too late.

Darko's anchoring fingers tear loose—and he's gone. He screams and falls, arms and legs spread in a black X, and then he's vanished, swallowed by the cloud and snow.

Danny sinks down on his haunches—his mind suddenly numb with cold and shock and exhaustion. The terror of that fall . . .

The lightning flickers again, lighting up the inside of the clouds.

So very cold up here and still climbing. Could be struck by that lightning at any minute. If that doesn't happen, he's going to die of hypothermia . . .

He's breathing hard, trying to control the shakes taking hold.

The darkness enfolding him.

How high will the thing go? Escaping its own shackles, escaping the earth, escaping gravity . . .

Fingers are numb already . . . Can't feel his toes . . .

He slumps down in the basket—and then he sees the sign. In the middle of the gondola is a basic control panel and the words *BEIM NOTFALL: GASFREILASSUNG*. A red switch below it.

Always have to press a red switch, he thinks numbly. And crawls over and presses it with his blue, shaking fingers.

From overhead comes the hiss of escaping gas. Escaping.

Exhausted, crouched in the bottom of the gondola, he doesn't feel the balloon sinking—but he does feel the first crunch as it strikes the tops of the trees in the Tiergarten.

And then there's the roaring, ripping, crackling plummet through the lower branches, the trees taking the impact of landing, the *sssssssshhhhhhhhh* as the fabric and its map of the world is ripped to shreds. The gondola strikes a tree trunk and tips violently, catapulting Danny clear. He takes a glancing blow to his shoulder, twists in the air and lands, face-first, frozen, bewildered in the snow.

For a minute he lies there, thinking nothing.

Then he rolls over onto his back, feeling the snow falling softly on his face. *Everything falls in the end,* he thinks. *Isn't that what Darko said . . .*

And then he hears a voice.

"Oh my God, oh my God! *Bello!*"

Danny Woo lifts his head and opens his eyes.

And there before him, blinking through the tumbling snow, is the single illuminated word *MYSTERIUM*—and Rosa hurrying toward him.

32

WHEN BIRDS TAKE FLIGHT

Zamora's funeral takes place a week later.

What's left of the company gather in winter sun-shine in the graveyard where Mum and Dad are bur-ied, the last of the early snow melting away, birds on the feeders in the bare trees, blue sky cut sharply overhead.

The plot is near Harry and Lily's, and gathered around it are Rosa, the Aerialisques in their black-feathered wings, Frankie and Billy, the Klowns in white suits, Inspector Ricard. Max, his hand heavily bandaged, stands with Laura.

And Sing Sing and Danny stand arm in arm.

The last week has passed in a barrage of police reports, hospital appointments, hours spent sitting in the big top trying to make sense of things, talking to Ricard, or simply staring at nothing.

The Forty-Nine is routed. Most of the section heads have been arrested, some killed in the control room firefight, a few in the hospital. Darko's broken body was found a day later in a patch of waste ground, identified by Aki who volunteered for the job, and then taken away to the police mortuary.

Max and Laura stood huddled in conversation, swapping notes with Ricard, putting bits of the puzzle together. Danny had listened, contributed what he could—but the gaps in their pooled knowledge (Dad's activities, La Loca, the death of Darko's father) still yawned wide.

And what does it matter anyway? Beyond a mystery there's always another one waiting, Dad said. And beyond the grief, more immediate worries are piling up. What will happen to him now? Back to moldering away at school in England, putting up with Jamie Gunn and his stupid bad-guy act? Some other school, starting all over again? That would be like going backward—surely he's outgrown all that. Laura has brushed his questions aside, wrapped up in writing her news story.

"We'll have to see," she said. "You're not even thirteen for another month. Let's just be glad you're alive, huh?"

"But I want to stay with the company."

"Who knows if there's even going to be one?" Laura said with a sad smile and turned back to her laptop. "We'll get home, see how bad the damage is at my place since Darko's goons ransacked it, and then make a decision."

Now the small wicker coffin rests by the graveside, bowler hat placed reverently on top.

Danny can't pull his eyes from it.

In it lies the best friend he's ever had. The man who saved his life. The strongest, noblest person he has ever known. The rock of the Mysterium. Danny keeps thinking of writing those words on Zamora's arm cast a few days ago, and his eyes blur the image in front of him. No holding the tears now.

Rosa has improvised a few words and talked about Dad and Mum, the Mysterium, about Zamora's life and qualities. She finishes with the words: "He was bigger than any one of us"—and then breaks into a sob. Now they're all standing in silence, letting the birdsong and quiet do the work, letting *that* say what can't ever be said.

The birds suddenly take flight from the feeders. There's movement by the graveside and the company part ranks to let a very short woman step forward.

A dwarf—with dark, wavy hair, stylish sunglasses, moving briskly on her short legs, her face set firmly.

Rosa looks up. "Gala! You made it. We're so very sorry." The woman smiles sadly, nods, and then walks up to the coffin. She rests her hand on it, her eyes welling with her own grief, and Danny turns away, remembering Zamora's heartfelt plea for a "bit of privacy."

His eyes fall on Mum and Dad's grave and he walks over to it.

The infinity symbol scrolls across the divided halves, joining them together, and he bends down in front of it, marveling at the light spilling through the acrylic ball set in the top. He moves his face so that the glowing beams play across his eyes.

A hand touches his shoulder, and he looks round to see Sing Sing. Her presence—her friendship—so welcome. "You OK, Brother?"

"No. How about you?"

"Just feel so sad." She sighs and lets the birdsong fill the silence for a moment. "And I really hoped we might get some more info about Mum and Hong Kong. Guess I'll have to try elsewhere. Maybe I'll pick up that thread back home."

"I'll help you. If I can—I promise."

That's another thought that's hard to bear: the strong possibility that—for now—they will be separated.

She smiles, as if guessing what he's thinking. "They'll have a hard job keeping us apart, Brother."

Danny looks back at the stone in front of him.

"What are you thinking about?" Sing Sing asks quietly.

"Just that I want to keep doing what Dad said we should do."

"And what's that?"

The morning light is clear on Danny's face as he turns, the green and brown of his eyes shining.

"Keep the wonder and mystery alive, of course. No matter what happens."

There's the stutter of firecrackers nearby.

Staccato explosions rip up the silence, sending the birds up from the bushes. Smiles amongst the tears by the graveside. The white-clad Klowns have lit long strings of noisemakers and are throwing them up into the clear air—and then the company are linking arm in arm and beckoning Danny to join them.

EPILOGUE

Two years later . . .

It's a spring morning somewhere on the outskirts of Rome, the seed fluff from the poplars floating down in the warm air as Ricard gets from his car, stretching after his long drive from Interpol headquarters.

Ahead of him, standing proud against the blue sky, is the great dome of the Mysterium's new hemisphere tent. It looks like a huge globe.

On the far side of the camp he can see Aki pushing a baby's stroller across the bumpy ground, and now Rosa's stepping from her caravan, hair wrapped in a towel, a rude song half out of her lips. Seeing the Inspector, she stops mid-syllable, smiles apologetically, and points toward the tent.

New lettering glows on its side: *MYSTERIUM REDUX!*

"Daniel's in there, Monsieur."

Ricard smiles and walks toward the entrance. Inside, the darkness is pricked by a hundred tiny revolving spotlights, a haunting tune floating down from the speakers high under the hemisphere. Maria's voice falling steadily to a cello accompaniment.

It takes Ricard a moment to get his eyes accustomed to the low light. And then he sees the young man leaning against the rigging, eyes trained on the spotlit high wire overhead.

"There you are!" he calls.

The figure turns and smiles. He's younger than his confident posture suggests, but still definitely older than the boy Ricard remembers. The half-smile on his face is that of someone doing what he should be doing. Something he was born to do.

The smile of someone who has found his home.

Daniel reaches out and shakes Ricard's hand firmly. "Monsieur Ricard."

"How are you, *mon ami*?"

Daniel points up at the wire. "Shhh! Look!"

A tall, elegant girl—Sing Sing—steps into the spotlight, out onto the wire, a fan in her upstretched right hand for balance: bouncing, dancing her way across the arena.

As she goes, the music changes gear, starts to pulse with urgency, filling the space under the taut ceiling of the hemisphere.

Perfect balance and poise as she moves to the music. And then the snow starts to fall. A steady downdrift of large fake flakes that seem to material-ize from out of nowhere, filling the air, falling past the fragile figure on the wire.

It takes Ricard's breath away—and for a moment he forgets the question poised on his lips, as he stares up at the spectacle above his head.

And then the music dies and Sing Sing has reached the far platform and is looking down at them.

"How was that, Mister Director?" she calls.

"Pretty good. We'll go again in ten minutes."

Daniel turns to Ricard and smiles, his eyes wide open. "Suppose I said I know what you're going to ask me . . ."

TIME IS A CIRCUS, ALWAYS PACKING
UP AND MOVING AWAY.

—*Ben Hecht*

AUTHOR'S NOTE

In some ways I was an odd child. (Aren't we all?) Granted, I loved football, climbing trees, war stories, but I was preoccupied—almost from the start—with "the big questions" of life: When did time begin? Where does space end? What happens after we die? Is there a God?

And frequently, as I explored the countryside round our house, I was shaken to the core by moments that felt as if they carried a peculiar and intense mystery in them: starlings pulsing into the darkening woods, the sunset behind the strange round hills that were old coal mining waste dumps, the silhouetted wreckage in an aircraft "graveyard" near Manston Airport.

They were scary—but also thrilling—and made me feel as if I were standing at the very edge of a fathomless drop—or about to cross that void on a tight wire, like Petit or Wallenda.

It was only later, when I studied the philosophy of religion, that I discovered there was a technical term for this feeling: *Mysterium Tremendum et Fascinans*—Latin for "a terrifying and fascinating mystery"—and that similar feelings had inspired numerous religious and creative thinkers.

Great moments in circus are metaphors for the fragile mystery and beauty of being alive—and that's why the company that Danny loves so much is called the Mysterium.

ACKNOWLEDGMENTS

I'd like to offer heartfelt thanks once again to "Team Mysterium." In particular . . .

At Hodder Children's Books: my forensically attentive editor, Jon Appleton, for his patience and humor—and to everyone who has backed this trilogy with belief and energy.

At David Godwin Associates: Kirsty McLachlan, my wonderful agent—always calm, always supportive.

In Berlin: *vielen Dank* to Oliver Reichard, for accommodation and for helping with research.

On holiday: all the "Moosetouriers," for happy Naudy memories.

At home: my wife, Isabel, and to my two sons, Joe and Will, who probably still don't know how much I value their love and wisdom.

And finally, thanks to both my parents—(Dad, I wish you could see this!)—for creating a childhood setting that allowed the wonder to shine—and which, at times, made growing up rather like being in the Mysterium.

ABOUT THE AUTHOR

Julian Sedgwick is an author of children's books who lives in England with his wife and two sons. Julian's lifelong interest in the arts and culture of China and Japan has influenced much of his work, as has his fascination with performance, street art, and the circus.